James Alexander Kelvin
(JAK)

VOYAGES ON AN INLAND SEA

Book One
of
The PETASOS Trilogy

Limited Special Edition. No. 20 of 25 Paperbacks

James Alexander Kelvin (known as JAK to his friends) is a retired professional who has lived in Glasgow all his life. Now free to pursue other interests, he has turned his hand to the writing of fiction. He still finds time, however, to travel, to read, and enjoy both playing and listening to music.

James Alexander Kelvin
(JAK)

VOYAGES ON AN INLAND SEA

Book One
of
The PETASOS Trilogy

AUSTIN MACAULEY PUBLISHERS™
LONDON • CAMBRIDGE • NEW YORK • SHARJAH

A CIP catalogue record for this title is available from the British Library.

ISBN 9781528909938 (Paperback)
ISBN 9781528959438 (ePub e-book)

www.austinmacauley.com

First Published (2019)
Austin Macauley Publishers Ltd
25 Canada Square
Canary Wharf
London
E14 5LQ

"The sea is as near as we come to another world."

North Sea off Carnoustie (1977)
Anne Stevenson

Help with Words and Names

Rothesay:	**ROTH**-say. The principal town on the Isle of Bute
Montague Street:	**MONN**-tah-gew Street. The main shopping street in Rothesay
Boatie:	a small boat
Balloch:	**BAH**-loch. A small town at the southern edge of Loch Lomond
Balmaha:	**BAHL**-ma-**HA**. A hamlet on the east side of Loch Lomond
Loch:	Lake
Blether:	talk, or chat
Sara:	**SAH**-rah, *not* **SAY**-rah; an old lady who lives in Balloch
Stradivarius:	a famous make of violin
Amati:	another famous make of violin
Fey:	**FAY**, having the second sight
Tricoteuses:	women knitting at the base of the guillotine, counting heads
Bad speak:	to speak ill of
InchPrior:	Inch-**PRY**-or. A beautiful island on Loch Lomond, now uninhabited
Faerie Isle:	An imaginary islet, a portal to the Land of the Fair
Skedaddle:	skee-**DADDLE**. To flee in an undignified manner
Fairlinn:	fair-**LINN**. Another name for the Land of the Faerie Folk
St Kenna:	abbreviation of St Kentigerna, an Irish saint, buried on InchPrior 8th century CE.
Petasos:	The winged hat worn by Hermes

Chapter 1

Shortly after breakfast, Rab and his Granda set off from their lodgings and walked along the seafront to the centre of Rothesay. The family had taken rooms in a boarding house for two weeks during the summer—their annual holiday away from the grime and the bustle of industrial Glasgow. Rab was glad that his grandfather had come along with them, as his parents spent most of their time arguing with each other. Paradoxically when left in their company, he could feel quite alone and isolated. By way of contrast, Granda was fun!

Rothesay was as fine a seaside resort as could be imagined, with splendid buildings and a glorious promenade stretching along the edge of the sea. Magically, the waters of the Gulf Stream warmed the climate here, and there were palm trees growing in the open air along the shore. It was affectionately nicknamed *'Madeira on the Clyde'*, despite sitting at a latitude close to that of Moscow.

The views out of the town were spectacular too, over the sea to mountains and sky—that is if the deadpan cloud cover typical of Western Scotland did not close in too much. Today the clouds climbed in massive battlements into an otherwise blue sky, giving alternating periods of sunshine and shade, the latter with the threat of an occasional shower. If they just remained mindful of the possibility of rain, it was altogether a good day for a little walk and a good day to spend a bit of time together.

As they progressed along the seafront, the town began to wake up in anticipation of the day-trippers who would soon be piling off the boats which regularly criss-crossed the Clyde estuary. Several steamers were even now moving in on the pier, waiting in turn to disembark their passengers. On some days, there was such a quantity of river traffic that across the water a haze would develop, created by so many vessels pumping their black smoke up into the atmosphere. Today that had not happened yet, although who could say what might come later.

Their little journey had a special purpose, and you could feel it in the determination of the way they walked—nothing overstated in any way, but purposeful nevertheless. At one point they made a sharp turn, walking up a short side alley into Montague Street, the main shopping area in the town. This ran parallel to the seashore, but with the big Victorian hotels sitting between it and the sea it felt quite contained and sheltered from the wind and rain which could sweep in at times.

They stopped at a shop with a large window facing the street. It specialised in all the things that you might need at the seaside—large inflatable multi-coloured plastic balls, skittles, flippers for swimming, and so on. However, it was not for any of these that they had come. A far greater prize was in their sights!

Sitting right in the middle of the window, and raised up to the eye level of an adult rather than that of a child, sat a magnificent model of a J-class yacht. It was a good size, and the detail was exquisitely crafted. Granda drank in the beauty of the vessel with his eyes and thought of his days working in the shipyards of Glasgow when everyone knew every ship that was being built on the river, whether in their own yard or in someone else's. What a splendid thing she was!

This was still not what they had come for, though.

Lower down in the window, at child level, were more modestly scaled toy sailing boats—for mariners of a much tenderer age! While Granda was momentarily lost in his reverie, Rab ran his eye quickly along the row of little vessels until he came to a yacht with a green hull and pure white sails. On an earlier visit to the shop window, he had fallen in love with this simple wooden boat and its uncomplicated design. He was not due to start school for the very first time until the end of the summer, and there was still innocence in the way that he saw life, uncontaminated by anything that resembled sophistication of any sort. In his imagination, this little boatie could be a pirate ship, a racing yacht, or a *man o' war*—perhaps even a great treasure galleon on her way back home from a mission to some exotic land!

This was to be his special present from his Granda, who had skilfully extracted agreement, if not outright *approval*, from the boy's parents to let him buy the child a wee something to keep him busy over the holiday. Rab had already decided what to call her, but just for the moment, this would need to remain a secret. Someone might steal the name he had chosen if they heard it before the boat was safely in his possession, would they not? Better safe than sorry.

With each of them lost temporarily in his own little dream world, time seemed to stand still. Their breathing slowed almost to a stop. Suddenly, Granda stiffened slightly, his eyes still on the shop window. He looked long and hard at whatever was being reflected in the glass and then let out a long slow sigh. He half-turned, then seemed to think better of it and returned to his original position facing the window. Rab caught the movement though, and spun around to see what if anything was there.

Across the street, a man was standing in a doorway, watching them carefully. He was dressed in country tweeds and had a deerstalker hat on his head, one that sported two little crossed feathers on the front. He was handsome and well groomed, but there was no expression on his face, and he did not move. Rab turned back to his grandfather, still watching the stranger mirrored in the window of the shop.

"Granda," he said, "who is that man?"

"Oh, you see him too! Is he still there? Have you seen him before?"

Rab turned, but the man had gone. Slowly, Granda also turned, and then looked back at the window. This time there was nothing there but the boat models to see. They both stood quietly for a while and then steadying himself, Granda took Rab by the hand, opened the door of the shop and walked in.

A short time later they both came out, Rab clutching a little green boat with snow-white sails. In his turn, Granda held a brown paper bag, which he slid into a satchel that he had been carrying over his shoulder since they had left their digs. This already contained a thermos flask and a biscuit or two, and he decided that it was time for a little rest after their exertions! Too much excitement could tire out a small boy, and they still had the rest of the day to face.

They returned to the promenade and found a quiet corner where they could sit overlooking the sea. Granda poured them each a little plastic cup of sweetened tea and added some milk stored in an old small brown medicine bottle that was kept just for this purpose. He ceremoniously handed Rab a biscuit, and together they munched and sipped away happily together.

It was at such times that they felt most comfortable with each other, not speaking but just sharing the bliss of a moment or two sheltered from the noise and distractions of the world at large. They both greatly valued this special friendship that can exist between grandfather and grandchild, a relationship as pure and profound as could be imagined. Neither one of them really thought about it too hard or tried to analyse it in any way of course, but they just quietly enjoyed each other's company and friendship nevertheless.

When they had finished, and Granda had managed to put all of their bits and bobs back into the satchel, they sat a little longer to watch the comings and goings of the ferryboats. Rab could not read yet, but he had learnt to identify the different steamers by their shapes and their company colours. It was a good few years now since the end of World War II and the wartime grey in which the older ships amongst them had previously been painted had now been replaced with bright liveries. Some of them were quite famous—the paddler *Jeannie Deans* (Rab's favourite), her sister ship *Waverley* (Granda's favourite), *Queen Mary II*, the *Duchess of Hamilton,* and so on. Rab's eyes were keener than his grandfather's, and he was able to spot the vessels from a greater distance. Not for the first time did Granda feel that he was getting old.

A shower of rain splashed down, and they fled to a nearby shelter to wait for it to lift. There were rather a lot of people doing the same thing, and it got just a little crowded. Protectively, Rab held fast to his new yacht and stayed close to Granda—even at this age he was already showing signs of the discomfort in crowds that was to trouble him in later life. After a while, the rain stopped, and the sunshine returned. Holding his boat in one hand and hanging on to his grandfather with the other, Rab was quick to leave the unwelcome presence of the other people who had also squeezed in away from the rainstorm. He all but pulled the old man away and back again onto the promenade. Granda smiled.

"Hey! What's the hurry, wee man? What is it that can't wait a minute or two?"

He knew the answer, of course. "Can we sail *Snowdrop* now?" Rab asked.

"So, you've got a name for her, then?"

"Yes, Granda! It looks like the snowdrops in the park at home," Rab replied. "I like seeing them after wintertime."

Now, Rab could not have seen many winters and yet he remembered this pleasing image and associated it with his new acquisition. Clearly, he loved his wee yacht already.

"A good choice!" said Granda. "Now that we know what she's called, let's find a little spot to launch her, shall we?"

It was quite dry now, but over the sea, a glorious rainbow appeared, spun by sunlight passing through a million raindrops as the shower passed on its way. Granda and Rab watched entranced for a while until it faded, so caught up in the beauty of the moment that they quite forgot to go in search of any pot of gold—not that it would have been easy to find, of course, right there in the middle of the sea!

They made their way along the shore to an outcrop of rocks which jutted out into the water. Apart from themselves, there was nobody there after the heavy rain, and Granda was able to choose an advantageous location for their historic launch of *Snowdrop*, unconcerned about the presence of others. He reached into the satchel that he was carrying and pulled out the brown paper bag from the shop. Inside was a wooden frame that held a length of fishing tackle wound around it.

"See now, lad. Let's fix one end of the tackle to the wee hook in the bow of the boat. I'll hold the frame and let the line out slowly while you get *Snowdrop* into the water and point her out to sea. That's it! Now, watch what happens as she heads out."

The little boat sailed bravely out into the sea, watched lovingly by one small boy and his Granda—who was carefully holding the free end of the fishing line. When it was fully extended the tackle suddenly went taut, making *Snowdrop* stop dead and spin around to face back the way she had come. Granda gently rewound the line around the frame, and a few minutes later the tiny yacht came safely back to Rab. The boy lifted her carefully out of the water, the most wondrous expression of joy on his face.

"Oh, Granda," he said. "Thank you for my lovely present!"

"Remember that trick with the fishing tackle, Rab."

"I will," said the boy.

Granda smiled a secret little smile, and in not much more than a whisper added the words

"Remember me too, laddie".

Chapter 2

Loch Lomond was the largest "lake" in Britain—over twenty miles long and nearly five miles wide at its broadest point. It cut more or less due north-south, narrowing where it squeezed its way past the mountains on either side.

The loch had many islands of differing sizes scattered here and there, but there was one unusual feature of those farthest to the south. They lay in a straight line that followed the Highland Boundary Fault, an ancient rift in the earth's crust that ran from the east to the west coasts, separating the Highlands of Scotland from its Lowlands.

On the eastern shore of the Loch, just above the hamlet of Balmaha, the line of the fault rose upwards, forming for a moment a sizeable outcrop of rock known locally as Conic Hill. From its summit, wonderful views could be had out over the water.

Very deep in places—even deeper than the North Sea—the loch could be treacherous. Almost every year, or so it seemed, someone got drowned—usually dragged under by the strong currents that could surge beneath the surface. As an expanse of fresh water separated from the sea, it had no tides, but disturbances in the thermal layers down in its depths could cause strange upwellings. The consequent counter-sinking elsewhere of large volumes of water could catch the unwary, and pluck them all too readily from the world of the living to the world of the dead.

Today, though, the loch was mirror calm and reflected almost perfectly the enclosing mountains and sky—a kind of double image of itself. There was not a breath of wind, and it might have become stiflingly hot had it not been for the cooling effects of the water itself. On weekends like this, it was popular with day-trippers out from Glasgow for a picnic in the clean fresh air. The loch was stunningly beautiful in all seasons, and if you did not want to participate in the sailing, fishing, or hillwalking that it offered, it was considered quite acceptable just to sit quietly and enjoy the views.

Rab stood at the water's edge and watched *Snowdrop* as she tried to sail out into the loch. He had remembered to attach the fishing tackle as Granda had taught him the year before at Rothesay, but the lack of any breeze whatsoever had left the little yacht quite becalmed and motionless, unable to go anywhere. He knew that things could change rather quickly, though, and if he were unwary, a rogue gust of wind could carry the boat away from him with no hope of recovery. The fishing line was there as a security measure—a wise precaution on this most untrustworthy of lochs.

He missed his grandfather dreadfully, taken away over the winter months by the 'flu which had gone its usual rounds in the crowded city. There was nobody else Rab trusted or that he cared about in the same way, and he had withdrawn into a world of his own behind barriers specifically designed and constructed by himself to keep unpleasantness at bay. His parents didn't even seem to notice his departure from their own plane of existence, quite simply because they had never really acknowledged that he had been on it in the first place. They were always too busy trying to score points off each other to register anything very much that was beyond their immediate concern. Rab just shut out their constant squabbling and got on with his own thoughts.

A few yards behind him on the shore, other members of the wider family were preparing their *alfresco* lunch on a campfire that was backed up by a couple of primus stoves. About twice each year, weather permitting or not, a little fleet of their family cars went out on a Sunday to a local beauty spot—of which there were many—to have an open-air meal together and a good blether. Today, they had stopped at one of a series of tiny bays carved out of the west side of Loch Lomond, next to the road which headed north from Glasgow up into the Highlands. Other groups had adopted adjacent bays for the same reason, and on a good day, you really had to get out early if you wanted to find a half-decent space of your own to occupy.

Rab's Aunt *Lilla* (a nickname given to her when she was a child) was a delightful little woman who bounced around keeping all the preparations going. She could be gently forceful in a way that nobody could ever find offensive, as she was always careful to make a joke out of any difficulties that might arise and need resolving.

She was the only person who spotted that perhaps all was not well with young Rab, that he was seeking his own company rather more than she considered quite right. Like everyone else she had more or less given up on the boy's parents, so absorbed were they in their never-ending conflict. She had noted on previous occasions that neither his mother nor his father paid much attention to him and that he was uncomfortable in their presence. It was a crying shame, she thought, as he was a nice lad and she could see no badness in him that could warrant being shut out in this way.

Now that he was at school, the process of isolation from his immediate family seemed to be on the increase. Rab had already become bookish, and he seemed perfectly happy to be absorbed in a storybook or a magazine, rather than being out and about doing the usual boyish things. Not surprisingly his reading skills were developing fast, but there were times when he laid aside his book and simply looked off into the far distance, focussing on *goodness-knows-what* that he saw out there. In truth, though, he was never any trouble to anybody.

At only six years old, he was totally familiar with being ignored by those who were supposed to be his nearest and dearest. Attempts on his part to attract attention to himself earlier in his short life had invariably backfired, and he had learnt rather quickly not to do anything very much that would get him noticed.

Aunt Lilla was a lovely, warm human being with an infectious little laugh that was often used to cover over any social awkwardness she encountered on her journey through life. She was married to Rab's uncle, his mother's elder brother, and had two sons of her own—both a little older than Rab—who were growing up to be nice kids. They were no intellectuals, however, and took their pleasure in life exclusively from sports and games. It was an effort to get either of them to do any schoolwork, and she never—*just never*—caught either of them reading a book! Right at that moment, her boys were playing ball a short way down the little beach. She was well used to keeping an eye on them without actually seeming to do so, and was in fact altogether rather skilled at quietly observing and noting what was going on around her.

"Rab," she called, "would you not like a roll with sausage? They are just becoming ready to eat, and you can have one now before the rest of the tribe descend like gannets! Shall I put some sauce or mustard with it?"

Rab placed the wooden frame down on the beach and secured it with a large pebble. *Snowdrop* had still not moved, though. He turned to his aunt and gave her a smile that shone from his very eyes. It warmed her heart, as she only rarely saw an expression of any sort on his face.

"Oh yes, please!" he said, tickled pink that he had been asked first. He walked up to the campfire, and she handed him an open roll with a portion of flat sausage in it. She then took up a bottle of tomato ketchup and shook a little of its contents over the roll before closing it over.

"There," she said. "You can have some juice with it if you can find a wee place to put down the paper cup."

He took his little lunch and retired to a corner that had a boulder he could use as a table. Fresh air makes everybody hungry, and he was absolutely no exception! He set everything down, and briefly casting an eye in the direction of *Snowdrop* to check that all was still in order, began to eat.

Suddenly his father was there standing over him.

"I see that you've attended to yourself first, as usual, Rab," he said. "Don't worry about the rest of us. We'll manage on our own!"

He left as swiftly as he had arrived and picking up a couple of filled rolls, took them back to his wife. She didn't even look over in Rab's direction before launching into the next stage of her latest dispute with her husband. The boy was by now totally accustomed to this kind of behaviour, and with plenty of practice behind him buried any hurt he might have felt at his father's sarcasm in some deep place where it could be quietly forgotten— or not, as the case may be.

Aunt Lilla had noted the little exchange between father and son, and when she had an opportunity, slipped over to Rab.

"Are you enjoying your roll, Rab? There will be some more in a minute if you would like. Could you work in with me to clear up afterwards? I think your mum and dad would be pleased to see you help out."

What she *really* meant was that it might give them one less thing to criticise him for. Rab got her drift. He doubted somehow if his parents would even notice him 'helping out' as his aunt had put it. He liked her and trusted her, however, and was happy to go along with her suggestion.

Later, when she was going around refilling people's paper cups with tea, juice, or whatever else they were tippling, she paused briefly by his parents.

"I hope you don't mind," she said, "but I've asked young Rab to help me clear everything up later. I always like to make sure that we don't leave any litter behind."

And then, with one of her disarming little smiles, "It's good to see you all out enjoying yourselves," she said. "It must be quite a responsibility bringing up a gifted child. I admire the way that you give him a little space to himself. He's quite a thinker, that one, I feel." *And if you would just stop fighting for five minutes, you might find time to give him a little brother or sister. Well, not right here in front of everybody, I hope!*

They looked at her blankly. *Gifted child—who? Thinker! What was she rabbiting on about?* Ah well—whatever it was it wasn't worth bothering about, surely. Moments later, they had managed to find something else to disagree about—not that it took much effort.

Having made her point, but not at all sure that *they* had understood it, Lilla swept off and began to gather in all their refuse in a cardboard box. Dutifully, Rab helped her. He exchanged a little hello with everyone he passed and managed a polite smile whenever anybody looked his way. He didn't bother trying to do either, though, when he cleared away his parents' debris—no point in interrupting their loving exchanges (!) was there? Some hope!

Lilla took note, in her usual understated manner. *Maybe he's coping with it all just fine,* she thought. *Anyway, there's nothing much anybody else can do, except to let him know that he's liked by the rest of us. He's strong enough, in his quiet little way. I must pop around to his house from time to time to check up on him. I'll do it next week when I've made some jam. A jar or two of that is always welcome, and giving some to his mother would make a perfect excuse for a visit.*

When all was done, Rab returned to the shore. *Snowdrop* still lay at anchor in her imagined harbour, the crew fast asleep down below, waiting for a favourable breeze. Today, she was a clipper ship, carrying tea from China—or was that spices from India?—to be sold in the grocery shops of Glasgow. Her young captain surveyed his charge and wondered if she would ever get enough wind to send her on her way. *"Patience is a virtue"*, he had heard people say.

The faintest current of air began to ripple along the shore, and the little ship awakened from her slumber. Ever so gently, she headed out towards the great blue yonder, with Rab paying out the fishing line little bit by little bit. The adventure had begun!

Gaining momentum, *Snowdrop* sprang out into the loch. Just as she approached the farthest point that her tether would allow, a small rowing boat passed smoothly by, a man sitting alone in the centre. Strangely, Rab could see no sign of any oars—the boat just seemed to be moving all of itself. He took little notice, however, of the vessel's unexplained movement as something else caught his attention and gripped him tight.

He recognised the passenger in the boat from that day in Rothesay when he and his Granda had been looking in the shop window and had spotted a stranger watching them. This time the man wore an American-style baseball cap—it shaded his face somewhat, but still revealed enough to show how handsome he was. Just at the point when *Snowdrop* seemed to be trying to decide whether to collide with the rowing boat or to spin around and return to shore, the man turned towards Rab and for just a moment looked straight at him.

Rab froze, transfixed by two eyes the colour of deep sky, piercing him from within the shade of the cap's projecting skip. Above, and on the hat itself, a winged metal badge glinted brightly in the sunlight. Rab stood utterly still, mesmerised for a second or two until the man dropped his gaze and looked down at *Snowdrop*. Rab watched—it was all he was capable of doing—as the stranger reached over the side of his boat, gently turning the little green yacht around with one hand to point it back whence it came. With an almost imperceptible nod of his head, he then glanced briefly at the boy, only to turn away as his boat continued on its way.

Rab felt numb but slowly began to recover his composure. He looked quietly out over the water as the rowboat began to disappear behind the next little headland. As it vanished completely out of sight he drew in a deep breath and turned to see if any of his family had noticed anything. Not even Aunt Lilla seemed to have been aware of the silent little exchange between the boy and the stranger in the boat.

In the next little cove, only a few yards away, another group of visitors to the loch was laughing and playing with shuttlecocks and beanbags by the edge of the water. A girl in a pale blue swimming costume was splashing about rather clumsily, trying out what she cheerfully considered to be her various swimming strokes. She wore a white bathing cap, so it was not possible to see either the length or the colour of her hair. She had not yet begun to blossom physically in the way that young girls inevitably do, but this was probably going to be the last year when she could disport herself in this manner in front of males without attracting greedy glances.

She decided that she wanted to practise her dives, so she positioned herself on a little rocky outcrop a few yards out into the water. She plunged in headfirst several times, then turned to do the same on the other side of the rock. This time she did not come back up.

No one seemed to notice anything for a little while, and then there was a scream from one of the other youngsters as she gradually floated facedown up to the surface. There was a stain of red in the water around her head. Immediately, there was a commotion, as men rushed into the water to bring her up. It was too late. She had struck her head on a submerged rock and died immediately. The killer loch had taken another victim.

One or two of Rab's party dashed over to see if they could help, but in truth, there was nothing that anyone could do. Aunt Lilla told all of the youngsters to stay where they were, and not to go over to the next bay. She herself realised that their pleasant day out was over, and she began to plan a discreet and controlled departure for them all.

Rab stood waiting for *Snowdrop*'s return—she just didn't seem to be in any hurry to come to shore. He hadn't been standing for long when the rowing boat he had seen earlier came smoothly back the way that it had come. The stranger was there, of course, but seated just in front of him was a girl in a pale blue bathing suit and a pure white bathing cap. They both looked straight ahead, and neither of them acknowledged him or registered awareness of him in any way. Wherever it was that they were going so purposefully, it was quite clear that it did not involve him.

Rab wondered if this was the girl who had just had the accident everyone was panicking about. Had somebody not said that she was dead? She didn't look terribly dead the way she sat upright in the boat. He wondered about this for a moment or two and wondered too about the silent exchange between himself and the handsome stranger. He was interrupted in his thoughts, however, by *Snowdrop's* return to harbour, quite exhausted by her exertions out over the oceans of the world.

Rab bent down to pick his yacht up out of the water. When he looked up again, the rowboat and its occupants were no longer to be seen.

Chapter 3

Glasgow in the 1950s and 1960s was a good place to get an education. The town council—or the 'Corporation' as it was known—took great pride in ensuring that in theory at least every child and every young person had access to good teaching and to the best of learning facilities. These opportunities were available in all publicly funded state schools, so nobody was excluded unfairly on the grounds of poverty or an unfortunate social background. As far as was humanly possible, *everyone* was given an equal chance.

It was all part of the old traditional Scottish value system, where it was considered higher praise to describe someone as *educated* or *cultured* than to refer to them as being *rich* or *well off*. It was somehow recognised that you might have acquired your wealth by any means imaginable, fair or foul, and it did not necessarily make you a better person. On the other hand, an education could only be obtained through hard work and was built on innate intelligence. If you were educated—and in particular had been to university—you were expected to conduct yourself in an appropriate manner and be an example to everyone else, rather than just go out and grab as much of the world's resources as you could for your own personal aggrandisement.

It was a noble ideal, of course, if not always a realisable one—and there were many who fell through the net for whatever reason. If circumstances were right, however, then it was possible to improve the mind, to develop it, and to gain an increased understanding and enjoyment of the world as a result. Many a working man or woman would come home after a day's toil and then go to the library or to evening classes quite simply for the joy of it, or to expand horizons—or both.

It didn't really matter to Rab whether his parents showed any interest or not. He took full advantage of what was available in his school and in his locality. His academic abilities had been recognised by his teachers, and he was able to discuss any number of topics with them when time allowed in the teaching schedule. They helped him to navigate the school's little library and encouraged him to pursue further reading in the much larger local public library whenever he could. As a result, his nose was rarely out of a book—and correspondingly his awareness and his understanding of the world increased exponentially, both at a physical and a spiritual level.

In one sense, it was something of a lonely journey—reading and thinking were not exactly social activities—but in another sense, he found himself able to relate to the thoughts and writings of a huge number of other human beings, alive or dead. *These* were his friends, his companions in life. He was *never* alone when in their company.

By now, his parents had actually managed to produce two more children, so they had even less time for him than before. Nobody else in the family apart from Rab had any academic tendencies whatsoever, so for much of his time at home he was left to his own devices, largely unnoticed in the general chaos of domestic life. He would have liked to develop an interest in music, but the constant background racket of parental and sibling warfare made this impossible.

In time, however, his parents decided that the growing family required a bigger home, so they moved out of the city to a small house with a garden—and more importantly from Rab's point of view, enough space to give him a bedroom of his own where he could work, read—and in due course, listen to the radio in peace.

This new house was in Balloch, a little town situated at the southern end of Loch Lomond. There were good public transport links into Dumbarton and Glasgow, and after initial reservations about going to live *'in the sticks'*, Rab found that he had no difficulty in maintaining his links with the city. With his growing awareness of the larger world, he did not feel in any sense isolated. In short, he had long since passed the stage when his mind could be imprisoned in any one place.

A near neighbour was a retired string player from the BBC Scottish Symphony Orchestra, forced to give up his professional career through rheumatoid arthritis. Rab cut his grass for him, keeping his garden tidy over the summer months and helping out in other ways as the man's life became increasingly difficult due to his growing incapacity. In return for this assistance, Rab was offered some free music lessons—an offer he accepted with delight. Thus began Rab's journey into yet another magical world—that of music!

Rab managed to acquire a battered old violin from a junk shop, and with a little help from the woodwork teacher at school, restored it to playable condition. It was no Stradivarius or Amati—not by any stretch of the imagination—but in due course, he became reasonably proficient at extracting a tune or two from it. While he was getting to that stage, though, he was banished by his family to the garden shed, where he could make as much scraping and squeaking noises as he wished without disturbing anybody!

At first, there was no focus to his musical taste, but with the expert tuition of his musician neighbour, he began to understand and to enjoy two different compositional styles in particular—classical and folk. Jazz and any other modern type of music left him rather cold, but the traditional music of his Scottish homeland on the one hand or the works of Bach and his contemporaries on the other absorbed his attention completely. That was enough to keep anyone busy, was it not?

In the privacy of his own room, he listened to his radio whenever possible. He found that he could read or study quite easily if there was some kind of decent music being played in the background. The hours doing school homework would spin effortlessly by if accompanied by melody and harmony, and the combination of a good book and glorious sound transported him to places that he had previously not even imagined.

Of course, all of this distanced him from others in his family even more than before, but by now it quite simply did not matter. In spirit, in education, and in understanding, he had left them behind a long time ago and although he knew how to be affable enough when required, his full attention was never quite with those whose company he was in. They thought him a bit *fey*, not quite living in the same world as themselves—they got that bit right at least.

His tried not let his mind become cramped overmuch by his home surroundings, but he did find the endless background noise an irritant. Why did people have to make such a huge fuss saying virtually nothing? From long experience, he was able to shut out most of the cacophony of family life, but it took energy and effort to keep it all at bay. On those rare occasions when he had the house to himself, he found it sheer bliss to put on the radio and let the sweet balm of good music float through from room to room. He began to find other distractions, though.

On his way around the town, Rab often passed the little harbour in the River Leven where pleasure boats were moored. He frequently stopped to admire the various craft that were there, and in time got on nodding terms with the boatmen and other workers there. It was inevitable perhaps that they would get to talk together, sharing the usual daily discussions about the weather or what was happening in the wider world. Sometimes, he would even help out with the endless shunting around of moored boats, or with other basic tasks. If it was turning out to be a fine day, and he had cleared away any outstanding chores elsewhere, he drifted down to the waterside and mucked in with whatever jobs needed to be done.

Rab found that he could relate to all of this really rather well, and away from the dead hand of his family, he began to enjoy a simple social intercourse that had been unknown to him before. He kept quiet about his interest in Plato or Bach of course (!) but he found that at a human level and in a way that was new to him, he was enjoying this human companionship set in such wonderful natural surroundings. It was all a bit different from his customary cerebral activities—only he did not see it so much a *contrast* as an *extension* of his awareness. The pleasure that he took in the company of others, however, did not extend to large groups of any kind. His were the more intimate kinds of friendship, his preferences lying in one-to-one conversations where there wasn't the distraction of too many people trying to crowd in on his thoughts.

He began to develop a sixth sense for local weather conditions and knew somehow when it was going to rain or snow, how long either would last and if it was something that he needed to take seriously or not. The more time that he spent in the countryside around Balloch or in mucking about on the boats on the edge of Loch Lomond, the more he became at one with this beautiful and mysterious place. On the days when he had a chance to go out on the water as an extra bit of help on one of the larger craft, he found that he could read the complex moods of this inland sea in a way that could sometimes be slightly disturbing to his companions. He learnt quite quickly to say very little on the subject—but it had already been spotted. There were even occasions when he was asked what this or that cloud over the loch was going to do, or what a particular disturbance on the surface of the water meant. He was puzzled sometimes that others did not seem able to see things the same way, as if to them it was not at all natural. It seemed natural enough to *him!*

In a small community like Balloch, everybody tended to know just about everything about everybody else. Although he was always made welcome by the people of the town, Rab could feel sometimes that they had grown just a little wary of him. It was never anything that he could define, but he was often mildly aware of a slight discomfort in their dealings with him. The reality was that they found him a bit of a mystery, his braininess and his strange other-world perceptiveness just a little off-putting. He loved them, though, in his quiet understated way.

As the years slipped innocently by, Rab's confidence in himself quietly grew, until it had become a great strength—to himself as well as to the very few people that he felt he knew and that he cared about deeply. On the other hand, his family had largely become merely those individuals he lived with. They shared practically nothing, and if Rab had yearned for their affections earlier in his life, he did not do so now. The world had become a bigger and wider place for him, and in a sense, this bird had flown the nest.

Now in his mid-teens, he found himself thinking more and more about his future. He explored options at school with the careers officers, who without hesitation advised a further education at College or University. He liked the idea in broad-brush terms but as yet had no clear ideas as to what subject he might wish to pursue. Rab was streetwise enough not to go for something that might make it difficult for him to earn a decent living—there had to be a practical outcome in financial terms so that he could support himself in some degree of comfort and maintain a state where he was not dependent on others. He was not greedy or materially orientated—and he certainly did not wish to become either famous or wealthy—but he did wish to be financially independent.

Even at this early age, he sought fulfilment in other, more mature ways—but he did realise that it all needed to be supported by a disposable income of some sort.

Chapter 4

The summer had been a fine one, and Balloch was busy with tourists. This kept Rab occupied doing all kinds of odd jobs that paid him a little here, a little there. It all added up, though, and he was pleased that he would return to school with enough change in his pocket, so to speak, to see him through the winter months when there were fewer opportunities to earn extra cash.

Rab had been working that weekend at the yacht harbour, moving boats around and doing general cleaning chores. It all made few intellectual demands on him, and his mind floated free on this or that train of thought. He almost forgot to stop for a little lunch—a sandwich and a soft drink were all that he usually needed—until he noticed a commotion on the main road bridge over the River Leven.

Curiosity, combined with the realisation that he was due a break, led him to climb up from the river to pavement level at the bridge. There was some kind of cycle rally due to start, in aid of a cancer charity, and participants had come in from all over the county to take part. Most wore fancy cycling clothing that sported the names of their clubs, and in general, they rode expensive racing bikes—all well out of Rab's financial league!

There was a throng of people lining the pavements on the bridge, while cyclists filled the space in the middle of the road in a solid mass. A ribbon had been stretched from one side of the roadway to the other, and a minor local dignitary stood ready to give an official—and no doubt *officious*—send-off.

Rab found a less crowded spot to occupy in a corner away from the main gathering of people and unwrapped his sandwich. He had only taken a bite or two when he noticed a motorcyclist on the other side of the road from him, sitting quietly on his bike. He carried a camera—like most people there—seemingly ready to capture whatever images caught his eye. He wore well-fitting black leathers, and his helmet was painted with a gorgeous pattern of windswept wings. Rab wondered just what that little ensemble must have cost!

For some reason, Rab's attention was fixed by this motor biker. With an increasing sense of unease, he realised that he had seen this man somewhere before, and when he had done so it had always been associated with a death. He struggled a little trying to remember any details, but he was certain that he was right. He stopped eating.

The visor on the biker's helmet was raised, and he looked intently at the column of cyclists as they headed off past him in a near-solid block. As his head turned to follow them, he caught sight of Rab on the opposite pavement, and momentarily looked directly into his eyes. It seemed to Rab that there was a recognition of some sort, an acknowledgement that they knew one another. The biker gave a little smile, nodded his head, and pocketed the camera away in some inside layer of his clothing. Rab noted that he had not taken any photographs with it—the camera seemed to be just a part of his overall outfit for the day!

For a moment, the biker looked like he wanted to talk to Rab, but with a glance at the stream of cyclists going by, obviously decided otherwise. He dropped the visor on his helmet, started the engine on his bike, and made to leave. As he did so, he gave a decorous little hand wave to Rab before sweeping off after the cyclists who were by now disappearing towards the edge of the town.

Rab took his unfinished sandwich and returned to the lower level down by the river, where he found a bench where he could sit. Looking out over the fast-moving water, he somehow managed to eat the rest of his lunch—although he took no pleasure in doing so.

Who was that troubling figure on the motorbike? Where exactly had Rab seen or met him before? His memory was clouded, but he was absolutely certain that they knew one another from somewhere, from some time and place he could not quite remember.

He sat for some time, trying to piece it all together but the more he tried, the less he succeeded. After a while, he quite simply gave up and tried to let it all go. The sense of unease, however, would not lift.

While he was sitting there, two cyclists went by on the opposite side of the river. They moved smoothly, but seemed to be freewheeling rather than actually working the pedals. Rab wondered if they had somehow missed the main group up on the main road—taking a wrong turning perhaps. They looked straight ahead, seemingly unconcerned about where they were, or where they were heading.

Behind them and moving at the same speed was a motorcycle with a rider clad in black leathers. Rab immediately noticed the elaborately painted helmet with its wings. When he was directly opposite Rab, he turned his head and raised his visor with a sweeping gesture. Rab found himself contemplating two intensely blue eyes—eyes which seemed to gaze out from a farther beyond than he could ever imagine. The man continued to look at Rab for a moment or two, then smiled just a little before moving on.

They *did* know one another, but Rab could not think how or why. He continued to sit unmoving on the bench as the little procession on the other side of the river travelled out of sight. Left on his own once more, he stared across the river fixedly, unable or unwilling to take his eyes away from the other side. In truth, he felt quite paralysed and spent.

"They said I might find you here, Rab. You're late taking your lunch today!"

A pretty girl sat down beside him. Her name was Anja and she was in the same class at school as himself. Her family were from somewhere in Eastern Europe but had settled in Scotland to live away from the strife that afflicted their homeland. Although they had not previously had much reason to speak to each other, she and Rab had started to develop a friendship from working together after normal school hours on the French language.

They were blessed with a native French speaker for their teacher, and she had offered to give extra tuition to anyone interested in developing their skills—particularly with respect to pronunciation and accent. She worked with them both on various aspects of her native language and culture, much to the betterment of their linguistic skills—and to their understanding of each other.

"Why are you staring over the river like that? You look quite pale. Are you feeling alright?"

"Did you see anyone cycling, or riding a motorbike, over on the other side just now?" he said.

"Of course not! There's no pathway over there. How could anything other than a tractor or an army tank get through? You *are* a little strange this afternoon! Has the sun got to you?"

He liked Anja, and already he was coming back to himself in the warmth of her company.

"No matter! It's nice to see you. What have you been up to today?"

They chatted about inconsequential things for a while, until Rab decided that it was time for him to get back to work. They walked along the towpath to the harbour, where Rab discovered that he was no longer needed for anything in particular that afternoon—often the way of things with his kind of work. In truth, his employer that day thought it would do the lad good to spend a little time with young Anja—she had a smile that could light up the darkest night, and Rab needed to shake off that air of seriousness that he always wore. Any chores needing to be done could easily wait until tomorrow!

Rab collected his dues and suggested to Anja that they got themselves an ice cream. They strolled around to the other bridge in Balloch—the one nearer to the shore of the loch—where there were teashops and ice cream vendors for the tourists. Rab bought two *'pokey hats'*—as cones were called in these parts—and asked to have some raspberry sauce trickled over them. They sat on a low stone wall, watching the world as it went by, chatting away about nothing in particular.

Suddenly, a ripple of shock ran through the people there, as word was passed around about an accident that had just taken place on the edges of the town. Apparently, a car had run out of control—slipped its gears perhaps—when trying to turn out of a side street, and had sliced through the tail end of the column of cyclists. Two people had been killed.

Rab felt sick. He had been right about his concerns when he spotted the motorcyclist on the bridge. He had seen more than by rights anyone should when he watched the two cyclists and their companion ride by on the other side of the river. He'd had no time to think about any of it, but he was deeply troubled by the whole experience.

He suddenly realised that Anja had caught hold of his arm. She had gone limp at hearing the news and was weeping softly to herself.

"Can we go and walk somewhere?" she said in a half voice. "I need to get away from here—*please!*"

Holding onto each other, they walked to the edge of the town park and turned in among the trees and flower gardens. Neither spoke. They continued walking until they reached the edge of the loch, and were able to look out over the water. There were boats of many kinds sailing around the headland, each coping in its own way with the strong currents caused by the outflow into the nearby River Leven. Some craft were beautiful, some were not. None seemed to be aware of the tragedy that had just unfolded back in Balloch. The two youngsters were left quite alone, and unnoticed.

After a while, Rab decided to take Anja back to her family. She had not spoken since leaving the little seating area where they had eaten their ice creams and was quite clearly still distressed. They walked, hanging on to each other as they did so until they reached Anja's house.

Without a word, she climbed the few steps to her front door and went inside.

Chapter 5

It was Maisie McFarlane's turn that night to host the Upper Balloch Ladies Knitting Circle. Although its exact provenance could sometimes be a little difficult to define, let it merely be said that the Circle was the closest thing you could find in these parts to a combination of the Spanish Inquisition and a witches' coven. Nobody's reputation was safe, and mere gossip could be turned into iron-hard fact in the wink of an eye. A more formidable group of *tricoteuses* had not been seen since the beheading of Marie Antoinette!

In truth, there was no such place as Upper Balloch, but the ladies definitely thought of themselves as being superior to *Lower* Balloch—wherever that might be exactly. None of them ever admitted to having gone down there themselves of course, but they had heard—had it on reliable authority even—that there were things happening in some parts of the town which were quite scandalous. A moral stance would have to be taken, and the Circle was the one to take it!

The ladies met once a month, rotating through their membership for a place to meet. Tea and biscuits were provided, and they would quickly settle down to an evening of discussing whatever had been happening since they last met. Knitting needles would be sharpened to a deadly point, ready for plunging into some poor soul's standing within the community. A suitable target for their disapproval would be selected and examined *in absentia* for misdemeanours, real or imagined. Dire warnings and predictions would be rehearsed until they had the force and authority of the Ten Commandments. Nobody was safe from their deliberations—except themselves of course.

Sometimes they even got some knitting done too.

Last month's victim had been Rab. They had been trying to find something scabrous to say about him for ages, but he had outwitted their manoeuvres and eluded them time and again. His technique for dealing with their assaults was actually very simple—he just couldn't care less about their tittle-tattle, and he consequently ignored their every attempt to blacken his character. It really annoyed them *no end* when all their very best efforts just didn't even seem to get noticed! He knew that of course, and it warmed his heart on cold nights.

This time they had gone too far, though, and some kind of retaliation was called for. Word had got back to him that they had inflated the story about Anja's reaction to the deaths of the cyclists that day when they had sat by the bridge with their ice creams.

Why, the girl had been seen clinging to him in public, and in broad daylight too! She had been quite clearly ill—morning sickness, you know—and he had spirited her away into the park to hide her from everyone. He probably got up to some more mischief in amongst the trees while he was there—well actually, it wasn't probable at all, it was a certainty! He had always seemed such a nice quiet lad, but then they were the worst kind, were they not? You never did know what they were thinking and maybe that was just as well—people, and especially young people, needed to be protected from that kind of person. How exactly was it you spelt 'libidinous' anyway, and did it not come from the same Latin root as 'libertine'—or was that 'libellous'? Rab was known to have an interest in the classics, and he had probably picked up bad habits from reading things like 'Imitations of Immorality' by that Lake District poet—what was his name?—English, anyway, and so not completely to be trusted. Anybody who could wax lyrical about something as silly as a bunch of daffodils was quite clearly half-mad anyway! When did everyone think Anja would be due, by the way, or would she have it terminated—hmm?

Rab considered borrowing a couple of nuclear missiles from the American Polaris base at Holy Loch nearby, and using the Circle as target practice. Best not to overreact, though, he thought—one missile would probably be enough!

He eventually decided on a more subtle approach. He had managed to find out that the Circle was due to meet at Maisie McFarlane's house. It lay not too far from where he lived himself, just a short walk up the hill. On the night of their meet, he trotted up to her door and knocked. Maisie was just a little taken aback to see him when she answered the door, but she could hardly ask him into the living room when the Circle was in full deliberation. After the hatchet job they had all done on him last month, however, she didn't want to be seen speaking to him in view of anyone passing in the street. She compromised by drawing him into the hallway, making sure that the door between them and the Circle was closed.

Rab knew these houses well enough, though, to be perfectly aware that that sound would carry without difficulty, so he was able to drop his voice, apparently conspiratorially, and still be heard.

"Mrs McFarlane," he said, "I've heard a terrible rumour that you ought to know about." The silence inside the living room was deafening as every ear strained.

"Down in the town it's being said that there are strange goings-on in parts of Balloch—the more respectable parts, that is." Maisie trembled with anticipation. She desperately wanted to hear this in private before anyone else did, but how could she?

"Yes," Rab continued, "they say that there's been wife-swapping going on up here. All the menfolk are conspiring to get their wives out of the house so that they can get on with—well, you know what! Now I think that's just a terrible thing to say. I was going to talk to the minister about it, but I'm not altogether sure that he's not at it too! What do you think I should do?"

Maisie picked herself up off the floor just in time to sidestep a stampede of irate women, all rushing past her on their way home to catch their husbands *in flagrante delicto*. Rab feigned surprise, flattening himself against the wall to avoid being crushed. Just loud enough to make sure that they all heard as they flashed by, he added, "Goodness, so that's how the men do it, is it? Get the womenfolk off to some function or another where they are all corralled safely. They really have it all well worked out! Oh, Mrs McFarlane, I haven't spoken out of turn, have I?"

At the speed of light, Maisie grabbed her coat and shot off to where she had been told her husband was going for the evening. *Poker, was it? We'll see about that! It's obviously a code for some hanky-panky.*

Rab quietly let himself out.

Chapter 6

Rab decided to lay low for a while after that—better to act daft than get too smart and invite trouble. Anyway, there were so many accusations and counter-accusations going around the town that his own part in it all mercifully got forgotten rather quickly. He was wise enough, even in his teens, to let the rumour machine trundle right by him and leave him unnoticed in some forgotten corner.

The women in the Circle now glared at each other suspiciously when they met in the street, and nobody seemed—well, *free* to host another meeting for some time. Their husbands all had a good laugh at the whole scenario—*chance would have been a fine thing*, they said! Mind you, now that the subject had been raised?

Rab well understood the saying '*no smoke without a fire*'. When he had the chance, he would nudge the stories along a little—and by now, there were plenty of stories—just to make sure that the flames of the imaginary 'fire' kept burning. After all his efforts it would not be in his interests to let that particular inferno turn to cold ash now, would it? He took particular delight in using the Circle's own weaponry against them—an innuendo here, a knowing little smile there—but nothing too obvious or explicit, nothing anyone could quite prove or disprove, nothing that could ever be traced back to himself. He knew how to act the innocent. Sod them!

With the Circle effectively rendered helpless, Rab felt free to pursue his friendship with Anja. He liked her, and she was the one person who could make him laugh. After school, they would often walk back together into Balloch town, along the banks of the river where they could get away from the noise of traffic.

Like himself, she did not much care for loud Western pop music. She preferred the sounds of her homeland, and would sometimes sing a song in her own language for him. He had to guess at their meaning solely from the rhythms and tonalities—and at times these were quite complex—as he could not understand the words. She teased him when he got it wrong, but at other times she was impressed by his insights into a musical world that came from the other side of Europe. His many trips to the concert hall listening to the music of Dvorak, Janacek, Bartok, Kodaly and so on, all allowed his ear to catch things that others in the West of Scotland might miss completely.

For his part, he had become sufficiently proficient on the violin to play really quite well—for an amateur, that was. His one-time violin teacher and friend had left Balloch to stay with family, finally to succumb to the ill health that had stalked him for so many years. Rab had subsequently been left to teach himself, but with the solid grounding in musical technique that he had acquired earlier on he was able to make quite decent progress in the areas that interested him most.

At school concerts, he did play Bach and suchlike composers from other eras and from other countries, but for Anja the most telling times were when he launched into the Celtic music of the west—music from the edge of the sea, music of the mists, music with the softness of colours that were washed by wind and rain. It flowed from him effortlessly, and no matter how often she heard his melodies she always seemed to be caught off-guard and surprised by their lilting beauty.

Anja had come to Scotland only a few years before, from a far land where many things were different. Whilst her family, whom she loved deeply, had in their hearts never really left their homeland, she had taken to her new country with its fascinating ambivalence of dark water and silvery light. She had absorbed her new surroundings so much that her spoken English was now indistinguishable from that of a local Scottish girl. Anja never felt any conflict in all of this, and in truth, relished the fact that she could experience and enjoy two completely different cultures, two different ways of thinking.

They had now entered their final year at secondary school, and the question of what everyone would do when they left could no longer be avoided. A few had decided on a university course of some kind, others on a less ambitious course at a technical college, while others yet again were still uncertain of where they wanted life to lead them.

For Rab, his academic leanings suggested some further education at college or university. His parents were completely indifferent on the whole matter, just as long as there was not going to be any significant financial input from themselves. He realised that whatever he decided on, the course would have to relatively short so that he could see it all through within a manageable timescale, and yet, he also needed to be capable of earning a decent living at the end of it.

He investigated the issues of student grants, looked at the availability of subjects he could study as close to home as possible so that travel times and costs could be kept to a minimum. He made his decision.

He discussed all of this with Anja, who knew and understood him as well as anyone could, if not better. She was supportive of his final choice and expressed enthusiasm for the quality of life that it could bring him. She herself, however, would not be drawn on her own prospects, as she knew that her time here in Scotland was coming to its end.

Her family had always wanted to get to America, and for them, the West of Scotland was a mere stepping stone on the way there. They had never tried to integrate into the life or the community of Balloch, in the way that she herself had done. Whereas things were substantially better for them here in their adopted country, it had never felt like home to them—perhaps because they had made no attempt to put down any roots, preferring ultimately to fulfil their aspirations in life on the other side of the Atlantic.

Anja had never really believed in their dream, seeing it as merely that—some kind of fantasy trip that would never become a meaningful reality. She had grown to love her life here on the shores of Loch Lomond, and quite simply did not care for the promise of greater material riches elsewhere. Young though she was, she saw all too clearly the lure of a false paradise. What was it they said here in English—*'the grass is always greener on the other side'? There was indeed such a thing as fool's gold*, she thought.

The choice was not going to be hers, though, and she knew it. One day they received the news that all of their paperwork—applications for visas, work permits, etc.—had been completed successfully, and it was possible to plan in detail to leave. Had she been just a few years older, Anja might have found the strength to refuse to go, but she was still attached by an umbilical cord to her kith and kin. She would have to leave with them.

The family made arrangements to move out of their home, and Anja made her farewells to those that she knew in Balloch. By far the most difficult goodbye she had to say was to Rab. Like herself he had known that it would come to this one day, but somehow he had hoped that it would never actually happen. Neither one of them had what might be called a teenage crush on the other—theirs was quite a different relationship, one that came from a human understanding that owed little to the sexual attraction on its own. Their friendship had become a close one, and they valued each other's company and thoughts. Under different circumstances, this might all have blossomed one day into a life-long love, but the circumstances here were *not* different.

They walked one last time by the river. They had discussed everything that they needed to discuss, and there was really nothing much left to say. There was a slight awkwardness while they reluctantly prepared for what promised to be their last moments together. They kept finding reasons to postpone their final goodbye. "I'll miss you, Rab," she said.

"I'll miss you too. Will you write to me?" he asked. She nodded, unable to speak.

Suddenly, he asked, "What will happen to Smozo? Will he be going with you too?" Smozo was her dog, a stray that they had taken in a year or so before.

Without warning, she burst into tears.

"There's no place for him in our new life in a big American city. My family doesn't talk about it, but I fear the worst. In a day or two, I'll come back home and he'll not be there anymore, I'm sure of it. It's how they do things—they think that it hurts less that way."

Rab thought he understood only too well what '*not there anymore*' might mean.

"I know of someone who might take him in—I would do it myself if I could. There's an old lady near where I live who's had a stroke, and she's effectively housebound now. She misses getting out and about, and people are saying that she should get a cat or a dog to keep her company. Unfortunately, she can't cope

40

any more with having to housetrain an animal, so it would have to be something that was already OK that way."

"How would he get his exercise? I wouldn't want him to become a prisoner."

"I could come for him every day. It means I can keep an eye on the old biddy as well. She will probably be pleased with the proposed arrangement, as I can act as a daily lifeline for her to the rest of the world. Shall we go and see her?"

Smozo moved house the very next day—just in time.

Chapter 7

Over the following weeks of the summer break, Rab was grateful for the opportunity to see Smozo each day. Somehow the dog provided a link with Anja—and for the dog too, Rab's visits eased its own abrupt change of family and home. The old lady was well pleased with the arrangement, as Smozo was very affectionate with her and seemed quite happy to sit by her side for long periods of time while she read the romantic novels of which she was so fond. Smozo knew that Rab would come around like clockwork each day to take him for a good romp in the fields or, if the ground was too muddy with rain, down by the river where the paths were semi-paved. He looked forward to that!

Rab always made sure that the dog was well exercised, and took a ball and a doggie-pull with him in a little rucksack for games while they were out together. Smozo liked to be stretched, so to speak, but there came a point where he was ready, grateful even, to get home to his new owner. She, in turn, always made a little fuss of him when he arrived back—just so that he knew that he was welcome in his new home. The beast loved it all of course, and so did she!

Without the dog, Sara could all too easily have become rather lonely and isolated. There were carers who came around regularly to see to her needs of course, and to make sure that she didn't want for anything, but they were busy people and hadn't much time for a chat. Similarly, the Scottish SPCA visitor who looked in from time to time to check on Smozo—a rescue dog living with a semi-invalid—couldn't stay for long either. The girl couldn't help but note, however, just how well cared for the dog looked—lean and fit, and always clean and brushed.

This last bit was their secret weapon with Smozo. After each of their walks together, Rab dried and rubbed down the animal if it had been raining, and then produced—wait for it—the *brush*!

With Sara looking on approvingly, Smozo got his fur combed out and untangled, all the time giving soft looks alternately in her direction and then in Rab's. Then it was time for a good snooze!

Although she tired more easily now, Sara always liked Rab to spend just a little time with her, chatting about the inconsequentials of Balloch life. Although she did have friends who dropped in from time to time to help keep her company, she also greatly appreciated the regularity of Rab's daily visits—the insights of a bright young person as opposed to the somewhat predictable views of her stuffy church cronies.

After returning from the daily walks, Rab would sit a short while, talking to her while letting Smozo know that he was being watched over as he settled down into his well-earned sleep. After five or ten minutes, Rab would bid her goodbye and then completely unnoticed by one exhausted but contented animal, quietly slipped away.

One day when they were out for their walk together, Smozo disappeared on Rab—he was there one moment and gone the next. After calling for him, Rab went on the hunt. After a fruitless search, he stopped for a moment and thought—*maybe, just maybe…*

Rab headed for Anja's former house and found Smozo sitting on the doorstep, looking perplexed. *Who were these strange people living there, and where was everybody else?* When he spotted Rab, he came forward and looked up into his face. *Well?*

Rab knelt down and pulled the dog close. Speaking softly, he told him that they had all gone now and were far away. He was sure that they were happy and had only left Smozo behind because he would not have liked living in a US high-rise apartment. Oh yes, and Anja had always adored him and no doubt would be missing him too!

Rab and the dog stayed together that way for a short time and then as one, they got up and continued their walk up into the fields. From then on, Smozo stayed close to Rab's side.

It was about a week later that Rab found out that Anja had disappeared. There were no details as to the precise circumstances, but it seems that it had happened around about the time of Smozo's visit back to his former home. Rab wondered about this—and wondered hard. The dog had shown concern, but not distress. He had gone to look for his old friend in her familiar haunts but had seemed reasonably satisfied when he found out that she was not there. What did he know?

They never did find out what had happened to Anja. Rab felt sure that she was OK, but if asked would not have been able to explain why. In the same way that he knew about the weather and whether it was going to rain or not, he could see that she was safe somewhere and content. That was all he knew, though. Everything else was hidden from him.

Smozo and Rab continued their daily routine as summer quietly faded into the beginning of autumn. It was close now to his start at college, so he had only a few days left before giving up his various little jobs in Balloch. He had earlier promised to do a little voluntary work on the island of *InchPrior*, clearing away brambles and dense undergrowth to make space for other species to thrive there. Sometime in the previous decade, the island had been given special status, and they were now beginning to formulate a strategy for its conservation and care. Help was required on a whole variety of issues, and much of what was needed would depend on unpaid labour. Always conscious of the need to give as well as to take, Rab willingly gave of his time to help out whenever he could.

He took a tent and some supplies and set off to camp on the island for a few days. Smozo was allowed to come with him— as his own little holiday—and he sat proudly and happily with Rab on the bus going around to Balmaha where they could catch the small ferry boat for the short trip over to the island.

After the last day-trippers had departed, they seemed to have the island completely to themselves—Rab was certainly unaware of any other volunteers staying overnight there. The weather held, and mercifully they did not have to experience the misery of camping in the pouring rain. The dog snuggled up that first night in the tent, snoring softly and wrapped up in his very own blanket that Rab had brought along with him.

Others had come and gone over the summer months to help clear away the undergrowth that was slowly destroying the island in one way or another. Until fairly recent times it had been in use, but eventually it proved to be too small to be practical for modern agricultural methods. In time, it was hoped that with just a little care and attention, some kind of balance could be restored, allowing the rather special habitats on the island to flourish again.

The graveyard at the north end of the island, nearest to Balmaha, had already been cleared and the graves properly tended for the first time in years. Even the foundations of the old priory had been exposed to view. Rab came there to have a look around, but Smozo would not enter, preferring to watch and to keep an eye on his pal from the safety of the perimeter. When Rab was working elsewhere on the island, however, Smozo sat or sniffed around right by his side, fascinated by the work being done—for a little while at least until he got bored!

After their meal on the third evening, they were sitting by the little campfire watching the flames play out what was left of their brief existence. Doubts had been expressed about the wisdom of having open fires on the island, so Rab was careful to have only a small fire, placed on the open ground near the shore and surrounded and contained by stones that he had found. Suddenly the hackles on the back of Smozo's neck rose and he growled menacingly—loud barking had never been his particular way. Rab looked around, but could not see anything. He trusted the dog's instincts sufficiently by now to know that they had an intruder of some kind. There were no foxes or badgers on the island—not enough food for them to eat—and Rab had not noticed any other people there that night.

"*Rab,*" a silken voice said, "*come to us. We are waiting for you. Leave the dog, and walk to the edge of the water.*"

The very last thing that Rab was going to do was to walk away from Smozo! The dog didn't like or trust whoever it was, and that was good enough for Rab.

"No!" he said, "I'm going to stay right here. If you want me to see you, come over to the campfire."

"*FIRE!*" the voice sounded shocked. "*You are cruel, Rab, to deny us in this way. One day we will meet again, I promise, and there will be no fire—or dog for that matter—to come between us!*"

Then there was silence, and Smozo gradually calmed down. Rab let the last embers of the fire die away, and then retired for the night, Smozo close by his side. The dog did not sleep, however, but kept a watchful guard by Rab's side.

They left the island the next morning. On the boat back to Balmaha, Rab asked the ferryman about something that had struck him as being a bit strange.

"Nobody has ever told me about that small island just off the shore by the campsite, the one with the great stones on it," he said. "I don't remember seeing it when I've been this way before."

"*The Faerie Isle*! You didn't really see it, did you? It appears and disappears for no reason that we know, and not always in the same place. They weren't trying to speak to you, were they?"

They disembarked and Rab and Smozo sat down at a table outside the inn, waiting for the bus back to Balloch. He treated himself to a cappuccino coffee and a biscuit, with one eagle-eyed dog sitting by his side positively willing the last piece of biscuit to go into *his* mouth and not Rab's.

"OK, ask nicely now!" Smozo lifted his front paws and begged with all the doggy charm he had at his disposal. He got his bit of biscuit.

Rab's thoughts turned to the *Faerie Isle* and the possible connection with the voice that he had heard the night before. He had noted the islet more or less on his arrival on *InchPrior* itself but had initially found nothing much to feel concerned about. The water level in the loch could rise and fall by as much as ten or eleven feet at different times of the year, with rocks and small islands apparently cutting up through the surface of the water, and then sinking later without a trace. What puzzled him, though, that wherever he was, whatever he was doing, the tiny isle always seemed to be in sight, almost as if it were watching him. Nonsense, of course!

Most troubling, though, was when they rose on that last morning and struck camp. Rab double-checked that he had not left any litter or other items behind and when he was happy that everything was in order, looked up and out over the water. The *Faerie Isle* had gone!

Now back on the mainland, they sat a while longer by the shore at Balmaha until they heard the bus chugging along the road. Rab piled on board with Smozo and shoved his gear into the luggage space behind the driver. As they were waiting for the bus to leave, Rab looked down at the dog, and thought how tired the animal must feel—he was sure that his wee pal had not slept at all the previous night. Yet he had spent each and every day there dashing about like a mad thing, wearing himself out. Rab wondered about that.

They rattled around to Balloch, disgorging passengers here and there. Rab and Smozo clambered off near where they lived and went straight to Sara's house. When the door opened for them Smozo burst in, all wet black nose and furiously wagging tail, but after a short while went to his basket and collapsed into it without his customary brushing. He was exhausted. Rab put the dog's trusty blanket by his side and murmured his thanks to him. "I'm glad you were with me, lad," he said.

Now, Rab and the Sara were separated by many years, but they had developed an understanding of each other and were able to speak openly about many things—something that they both valued. She looked concernedly over at Smozo, who was by now fast asleep. "Is he alright? He seems very tired."

Rab told her about the unseen visitor(s) to their camp the night before, and how Smozo had not slept at all after that. He had no idea who it was, but wondered if it was some kind of supernatural presence—he didn't know what though. He also told her about the disappearing island, and how the ferryman had called it the *Faerie Isle*—the fairy portal!

She sat, a distant look on her face. "Quite clearly you have the *sight*, Rab. I've wondered about it at times when I've seen just how easily you and Smozo seem to understand each other. My mother came from the Outer Isles and was gifted that way, too. Here on the mainland, she learnt to conceal it, as people here felt uncomfortable with someone who seemed to be half in this world, half in the next. I'm afraid that I didn't inherit her talent. My younger sister Jenny has the skill, though, and when she comes to see me again I think that you two should have a little talk.

"You see things that others do not—am I right? I suspect that you have never had anybody to talk to about it, so it must all seem very confusing to you. It's said that at some time in the past the *Faerie* interbred with humans and that there's a rogue gene that surfaces in us from time to time. Your visitors last night would have sensed that in you, and been trying to call you home to them. Smozo obviously felt something too and didn't want anybody or anything stealing you away from him. You are right to be wary of them, Rab.

"They were once powerful, but have faded in many ways until we humans are often no longer aware of them. They seek to regain what they have lost by calling in what they perceive as their own. They are not actually malevolent as such, but they do have values that we would not understand—or even *want* to understand. I am not *sighted*, so have no direct experience of these things, but I often heard my mother speak to Jenny on the subject, passing on her knowledge and insights to someone with her own ability. I'm not too sure that Jenny really listened or understood though."

Rab began, just began, to comprehend many things in his life. He had always wondered why people looked at him strangely at times or found him odd. He found himself wanting very much to talk to Jenny.

Chapter 8

As chance would have it, Rab did not have to wait long before he met Jenny. Sara needed to go into hospital for a few days to undergo a routine examination or two, and her sister decided to come to stay for a little while—more for moral support than for any practical assistance that she could offer. For all her customary *sang-froid*, Sara was afraid of anything that had to do with doctors or medicine and could work herself up into a panic over a simple visit to the local surgery.

Jenny's presence in Sara's house also made the whole business of caring for Smozo easier, as he was not left abandoned and shut up in the house for the time Sara was away. Jenny could have dealt with the dog's walks herself, but she didn't know the area particularly well and was grateful that Rab continued his practice of regularly taking Smozo for his exercise out into open spaces where he could have a good run.

One of the days that Sara was in the hospital, she was to have a series of minor tests which would both occupy and tire her to the extent that a visit by her sister was to all intents and purposes pointless. Jenny busied herself instead with some shopping in the town—nothing too fancy, just essentials—and settled down to a good book. Like her sister, she enjoyed a romantic novel from time to time.

It was perhaps there that the similarities between them ended. Sara had always been the more sensible of the two, the more pragmatic and the more orderly in her lifestyle. She had trained as a teacher and had that 'schoolmarm' way of looking at life. She had never married, being perfectly happy with her lot as it was. Jenny, on the other hand, was the easier one to like. She had little sense of organisation, yet somehow managed to float through life in a unique muddle of smiles and minor disasters that in combination invariably had everyone flocking to help her.

When Rab came back with Smozo that day, she anticipated their return by getting a pot of tea ready. Rab was invited to sit for a little while—which he was used to doing anyway. She poured him some tea, and with her customary lack of protocol of any kind got straight to it.

"Sara thinks that you might have the sight. Is it true, or—as I suspect—are you unsure about it yourself?"

Rab nodded.

She continued, "I might be able to help, but it would be useful if you would open up to me a bit—you are closed tight against me just at the moment. Try to relax a little, and just think about trusting me with your thoughts. That's better!

"Well now, who's the strong one, then? You have it in buckets, my dear, but you've just not learnt to control it—in fact, you barely use it at all. It can make you ill if you keep denying it, you know. Let's start with thinking about your experience on the island the other week."

Glancing over her shoulder to make sure that she was not being watched—a lifetime habit, even when there was nobody else there—she dunked her biscuit into her tea. She hadn't had much time to enjoy the fruits of her labours when she sat bolt upright.

"Well, there's no need to shout! Oh, I'm not talking about you, my dear, it's *them*. They're using you as a conduit of sorts—they know that you're not actually listening to them so they are bypassing you to talk to *me*. Can you give me just a moment or two to find out what they want—I won't keep anything from you, I promise."

She remained silent for quite some time, gently supping her tea, and then spoke to Rab.

"You have great strength in this, my dear, but you have never really developed it in any way. That makes you a complete innocent to them, a huge resource that they hope to mould to their own requirements. That's what they're after! I also feel that they are afraid of you for some reason. They've known about you for some time and that you were always tantalisingly near, but it was only when you were alone on the island and so close to their dwelling that they felt able to contact you directly—except you weren't alone, were you? You had Smozo there, who sensed them even when *you* weren't able to. Normally, they are clever with animals and can influence them and their behaviour all too easily, but this one must love you very much indeed if he managed to hold them at bay.

"Ah, the fire! These ones are spirits of the water, and stay away from fire whenever they can. They have no defences against it. That and Smozo together confounded them, and thwarted their attempt to abduct you."

"Abduct me!" said Rab, "What do you mean?" Jenny looked thoughtful for a moment, her head cocked to one side.

"They wanted to take you into their world and turn you into one of them—or something of that sort. I don't recognise the images that I am seeing—it would be you, but not you, whatever that means. They want to own you, but I don't think that they know themselves just what that might involve. Oh dear, I miss my mother at times—she would have understood it all so much better than myself."

"Would they have needed to kill me to steal me in the way that you say?"

"Sort of! It depends what you mean by death—oh, my goodness! *OH MY GOODNESS!"* Jenny looked like she had just been electrocuted. She forced out the words.

"I had no idea that *HE* was involved! He is seriously annoyed that they tried to take you before your time. It was foolish of them to try to circumvent the *Twelve*—any one of those is vastly more powerful than all of the Faerie put together. They must have been desperate!"

Jenny started to shake. It was times like these that she needed her sister close, just to steady her. Rab took the chance to seize the initiative in the conversation.

"Who do you mean? Are you referring to the man with the wings around his head that I sometimes see—though nobody else does?"

"Ah, you've actually *seen* Him? Rab, I don't know what's going on here, but you need to be careful. This is all beyond *my* meagre abilities, and there is a larger game being played here than I'm able to comprehend. That you have survived this long without being seriously hurt tells me you are favoured in some way.

Not even bothering to ask Rab if *he* wanted any, she poured herself another cup of tea, this time adding much more sugar than was her norm.

"Yes, I know that you have probably felt the pain of many kinds in your life, but you are still being protected, you know, and are especially dear to the *Great Ones*. They seek to hide you from those who would harm you and will continue to do so as long as you co-operate with them. Do you speak with them at all?"

It was the first time that Rab had ever opened up on the subject.

"It's only the one of them that I see, and He has never actually spoken to me—although He has acknowledged me more than once when He's been here. I seem to puzzle Him a little too, and He looks surprised when He catches sight of me."

Rab had turned pale.

"Rab, I daren't try to communicate directly with one of *their* enormous power, not without a lot of preparation—it would burn me out! They obviously care about you and won't hurt you—it's going to be up to you to follow this one through. I can, however, offer a little advice.

"Keep away from the island where you saw the *Faerie Isle* out in the loch—it will only inflame the situation by coming so close to them, and don't even think of taking Smozo there with you! Despite what happened there before, he is vulnerable too. When you are either near the island or on the water elsewhere, carry a source of fire with you—a simple cigarette lighter would do, even though you don't smoke. If ever you hear them try to speak with you, light it up—they won't like it and will back off. Oh, what *is* going on here?"

Rab didn't understand any better than she did—and probably a lot worse. He turned to Jenny.

"It seems that these *Faerie* think only about themselves, and have no concern for humankind. If they have thought to challenge the authority of those greater than they are, then it must be an issue of survival for them. Why? Are they dying out?"

Jenny started to tremble again and looked most uncomfortable.

"Rab, this is all too much for me! I don't think that even my mother would know what this was all about. I think that you need to talk to your mysterious visitor if you can. He is known as the *Messenger* after all. If anyone can help you with this, it will be *Him*."

"I don't know how to call to Him. Do I pray or something? How do I ask for help, then?"

Jenny looked at him gently. "I think you just have," she said.

Chapter 9

There were some people who claimed never to dream. Perhaps they simply did not recollect their dreams—but dreamt them nevertheless. Rab was of their number. He had clearly been able to do so as a child—that much he could remember—but on entering his teens he seemed no longer capable of travelling off in his sleep to those fanciful lands that constituted the dream world.

Things now changed. After his conversation with Jenny and the opening of *another* awareness, he began to find that his nights were filled with imagery, with sound and colours, with strange thoughts and sensations previously unknown to him—or perhaps just not recalled afterwards.

After a few nights, it all settled down and became relatively coherent. People that he did not know or recognise, but at the same time whom he did not fear, came and taught him skills about how to use his mind in new and unfamiliar ways. During the daytime that followed, and in particular during his routine train journeys to and from Glasgow, he went over what he had been shown the night before. His found too that in his regular walks with Smozo—where the semi-hypnotic rhythm of his own footsteps calmed and soothed him—these were good times to let his thoughts soar free and out into the vastness of the cosmos.

In this way, his prayer for help was answered. Rab began to see and understand better the things that were greater than himself. For many years now, he had in his readings of literature absorbed the teachings and writings of the great philosophers and thinkers of the past—but he had admired them with his intellect, rather than felt them with his heart. Now he found that he could do both.

Music, too, which he had always loved and where he had frequently lost himself, spoke to him more powerfully than ever before. There were times now in the concert hall where he found himself utterly transported beyond the confines of the physical world, almost to the point where he barely had the strength to rise from his seat at the end of the performance and return home. He knew that music had always been there as a part of him, but he had not consciously realised before now just how huge a component it actually was—and could yet become.

In short, he grew! As the weeks rolled into months and beyond, he transformed from a careful and somewhat silent young person into something rather different. He was much more inclined now to take initiatives of various kinds, especially in simple human situations where previously he had perhaps been reticent and retiring. He found himself more at ease in the company of others, and much more likely to smile. He saw now that there had been a bitterness in the past in his view of the world—and yes, he saw the reasons for that too—but he was now better able to laugh it all off.

It was still the same Rab in many ways, but it was a bigger and better Rab!

He began to find that he could programme his dreams, if only to an extent. If there was something in daily life that involved his emotions or his feelings, where he needed an answer that intellectual thought alone could not provide, he would think about it while falling asleep and ask for clarification. During the night, there would come to him images and voices, initially sometimes a bit unclear, where the matter in hand was laid out before him in ways other than he had considered before. Only rarely were there easy solutions, but Rab came to realise more and more that many of the difficulties that he had experienced in life were as much to do with his own perceptions and actions as they were to do with the outside world itself.

He still worried about his experience on *InchPrior*, when he had been approached by the *Faerie*. What had that been all about? Had he made enemies? One night when he was lying in bed, he found himself thinking about it all, turning it over in his mind again and again. As he finally drifted away into sleep, he slipped quietly into his private dream world, a place where he now felt quite comfortable and at ease.

***

A great being had arrived in the lands of the *Faerie Folk*. His presence there caused them some consternation and fear. He called their leaders together and faced them.

"*Fair Ones*," he said, "why are you so afraid, as I feel that you are? You have started to step outside agreed bounds, and I can only think that this is prompted by a deep unease of some sort on your part. I sense your panic clearly enough, but I cannot see the reason for it. This can only mean that you are deliberately hiding your thoughts and feelings from me, for otherwise, I would have no difficulty in understanding what troubles you.

"You did not inform me of your intentions with that young man who is under my protection, the one you tried to steal away that night on the dark shores of the *Lake of Tears*. I am at my strongest there on the *Great Edge*, did you not know? The fact that you also chose to appear at the boundary of day and night—when I am at my most aware of the world and everything that happens within it—tells me that you have grown proud, or foolish, or perhaps you were seeking to attract my attention in some way. What is it that disturbs you?"

There was silence in the ranks of the *Fair*. After a while, they answered.

"*Great One*, we have become fearful of the world of Men. Once, we were happy and content with our lot, but there are changes now in all that we know; in all that we see; in everything that we touch. It becomes harder for us to understand our own place there. We weaken, and we fear that one day we shall be extinguished. Why have the *Mighty* done this to us?"

Their visitor considered his words.

"First of all, know that We love you as before. *On High*, We too are subject to change and must shift and move with the flow of time in order to continue to exist at all—the instant that this movement comes to a final conclusion is the moment that we will also meet our own end. Our innermost essence remains true to us at all times, but We recognise that not to change at all is to die.

"All that exists and that knows life has within itself the ability to adapt and to evolve. Inevitably that ability will lead one day to extinction, the ultimate transformation—but without life there can be no death, and without death or the prospect of it there can truly be no life. They depend upon each other.

"The *Great Cycle* continues, but the time frame it marks out has no real beginning and no real ending, for they are both connected to each other. You are a part of it all, even as *We* are. Do you not understand that? Weep for your past if you must and remember it in your hearts, but embrace your future too, *Faerie Folk*. Only you can determine and shape what you can now become!

"I will leave now, but remember that you are not forgotten by us—and neither are you despised or rejected. Use your great gifts to find for yourselves how to move onwards, for no one understands as well as you do yourselves the true nature of your being and the potential that it holds.

"Farewell—*and leave the one called Rab to me!*"

***

In the days to come, Rab pondered deeply on this dream—or was it really a dream? Perhaps it was a *viewing*, where he had witnessed something that had really happened in another place—in another time even. He actually wondered if the *Messenger* had been addressing the *Faerie Folk* at all. It all seemed just too relevant to Rab himself.

He had never really known for himself the simple happiness in life that he could see in others. He had always been aware of his intellect, and how this could differentiate him from the people around him—his family more than any! In an attempt to compensate for his isolation, he had withdrawn more and more into his books, into his music, into the deeper parts of his mind, to places where he felt comfortable. Of course, this had just separated him even further from the rest of humanity and made their simple *joie de vivre* all the more difficult for him to share.

Somehow the few friends that he had in life had managed to break through these barriers, perhaps because they also felt imprisoned within their own walls—due to illness perhaps or in the case of Anja, being *foreign*—and sought to penetrate them. Whatever the explanation, he had never known many people that he could talk to and relate to easily.

Then there was Smozo, of course! It was one of life's great mysteries how two completely unrelated species like humans and dogs could become such great friends. As he well knew, with one's nearest relatives there could often be very little understanding or sense of sharing, and yet, by contrast, a whole world of communication could exist with a supposedly dumb beast. Rab's experiences with Smozo on *InchPrior* had greatly deepened his admiration for the animal. Smozo had known in his own way what the threat from the *Faerie* meant, and yet he had ignored risks to himself in order to warn and protect Rab. Rab had never known that kind of loyalty from any of his own kind— but there it was in abundance from a daft wee dog.

He tried to consider what kind of creatures these *Faerie* might be. He had never seen any of them, only heard their voice. Smozo hadn't liked them, but why? What did it mean, *they were weakening*? He decided that during his next trip into Glasgow's main libraries he would have to do some research.

The following Saturday morning, he took the train into the city and headed for the *'Mitchell'*, an enormous reference library much used by researchers. By now, Rab knew his way around the book collections rather well, and he homed in quickly on the works that he wanted to read. As he had expected, there was a goodly amount written on the subject—mostly garbage! Once he'd got past stories of *Tinkerbell* in Peter Pan and had looked at enough syrupy depictions by Victorian artists to last him a lifetime, a darker side began to emerge.

Rab thought about this and eventually decided that the word *'darker'* was rather unfair, if not downright misleading. Perhaps the description could more accurately be understood as *'unclear'* or *'opaque'*—*'hidden'* even. These creatures seemed to represent forces of nature, or more accurately had the ability to manipulate some aspects of those forces. The ones he had encountered on Loch Lomond were clearly creatures of the water, but the other mystical elements of *earth*, *air* and *fire* seemed, equally, to have their own *Faerie*.

Some writers suggested that they were once ancient pagan gods who had been supplanted by the later and more powerful Olympians, and then in turn, by Christianity. Rab didn't feel that any of this was right. In his view the *Faerie* had never risen to, nor had they aspired to, the status of gods—but they *were* something apart. From what he had gathered both from his researches in the library and from his own experiences in the dream world, these were simpler and less elevated beings than any deity, and they neither shared nor understood higher values or universal truths.

He had already commented to Jenny that they seemed not to care for anything very much apart from themselves, and perhaps that was because they were not equipped to do otherwise. Although they were endowed with skills and powers which were quite wonderful in their own way, they seemed quite incapable of considering the implications and ramifications of their actions—they did what they did, and that was the end of it.

Rab went over in his mind the dialogue that he had witnessed in his dream. If he understood it all properly, the *Faerie* did at least seem to realise that they were being left behind in this modern world of machines, of science, of learning—a planet now dominated by humans and not by themselves. Their own values—those of a raw and untamed nature; those of mystery and magic—seemed of less importance than before. In short, the *Fair Folk* felt increasingly irrelevant and unwanted. As they themselves had said, they feared extinction here. The *Messenger* had told them, however, to look to their own future—but not to forget their past. Whatever could that mean?

At closing time, Rab left the library and made his way home to Balloch. He stopped by Sara's house to take Smozo for his walk. As always, the animal was delighted to see him and came with him for his exercise just bursting with enthusiasm and energy. Rab was getting better and better at understanding the dog's moods—sharing them in a sense. Sometimes the two friends seemed to become so close that they were as one. Rab could feel Smozo's thoughts and reactions to whatever the beast was experiencing at the time, and Rab had become aware that in turn, his wee friend could tune in with unerring accuracy to his own moods, even if neither of them could fully understand the total extent of the other's thoughts. The connection was there all the same.

Later, he sat with Sara a little while. She claimed not to have the *sight*, but there was a clarity in her thinking that was just not evident in her sister's. Jenny had her gifts, certainly, but she could be overwhelmed by them and seem a bit scatter-brained at times. Whereas Rab had been grateful for her *insights*, he was not sure that he could trust her *judgment*—which was a different thing altogether. It was Sara he wanted to talk to.

"I've been at the library trying to find out what I could about the *Faerie*. You know about my dream, and I was trying to get to the bottom of it. I never will, of course, but at least I thought that I could understand them just a little bit better."

He then told her about his findings in the pages of books, and how so many ideas and concepts buried there seemed to contradict one other and to pose more questions than they answered. Sara had been listening carefully.

"As you have discovered, Rab, logic and reason are not strong characteristics in these creatures. Theirs is a world of instinct rather than of thought. If you try to understand them with your intellect, you will not get very far, I'm afraid. You need to approach this in a different way, and I feel that your dream explains the situation as well as can be expected. Theirs is a realm that is to be *felt* and *experienced*, rather than dissected and examined under a microscope.

"Yet for all these differences, they are clever with words and can ensnare you with tricks of meaning if you are not careful with them. You seem to have the *Great Dissembler* himself on your side, so they will be wary of you, knowing that you have powerful allies.

"My mother once said that the *Faerie* occupied a middle-world, somewhere between this existence and the one we all aspire to attain one day. If the spirits of the departed feel for any reason that they are not yet ready to make the complete journey, then they can dwell for a time with the *Fair Folk*. Their stay is only temporary and eventually, they must choose to leave—if they are wise—either to go forward or to go back. Quite why the Faerie allow this, I don't know. Perhaps they have made some kind of pact with *Heaven* to justify and reinforce their reason for existence.

"Too long in the *Faerie* realm will cause the soul to disintegrate and be absorbed into the very substance of its surroundings, usually to be remoulded into something that is a parody of itself in an earlier life. Their land is full of half-creatures who have not decided what they want to be or where they want to go. Theirs is the fate of those who do not wish to move on—in either direction!

"Yet ultimately they must make that decision, or they will find themselves expelled in their distorted state from this temporary refuge, to face their fate in the wider cosmos. Theirs would then be a truly terrifying existence!

"According to your dream, the Faerie did not wait for your soul to come to them naturally and in the fullness of time. They tried to snatch you away before you were ready. Your *guardian* was displeased and has reprimanded them for it. He has given them a chance to reconsider their purpose, and they would be well advised to take it.

"You are part of all of this somehow, Rab, but my sister was right to warn you to be careful. Listen to what you are being told, yes, and to whoever it is who is doing the telling—but keep your own counsel and adhere to your own values. Do not allow yourself to be used. Remain free."

On his way home, Rab reflected that even if he had not found many friends in his life, he had been extremely lucky in the ones that had actually come his way.

Chapter 10

It was one of those rare occasions in Scotland when the very best of astronomical and weather conditions managed to coincide perfectly, one with another. Often enough you could get them individually, but only infrequently did you find both of them acting in concert.

It had rained rather a lot over the last few days, washing the atmosphere wonderfully clean. The clouds that had been dominating the loch lifted away in the late afternoon, promising a clear night sky over the water. A crescent moon was scheduled to appear that evening and accompanied by the evening star, would be following the setting sun as it disappeared into the darkness beyond the western horizon. It would be a sight indeed!

Although there were a number of human settlements around the shores of the loch, these were not so many or so large that they would cause a major problem with light pollution. If you knew the area—and Rab knew it very well—you could choose a spot where there was, for all intents and purposes, no artificial lighting visible that would confuse or dull the eye. Now was one of those times where his knowledge would be put the test. He had already noted that there was to be a special event in the sky that night, and had seen to it that he was clear of any routine tasks that needed to be done. He pumped up the tyres on his bike, made sure that the lamps were functioning properly for his return journey, and set off.

He cycled around the loch to Balmaha. From his home, the road ran well back from the edge of the water and when he eventually burst into the little hamlet the loch was suddenly there, with the shadowy outline of *InchPrior* looming in the background. Keeping his back firmly to the island, he secured his bike on the edge of the car park and on foot began to climb Conic Hill where he reckoned the best views were to be had. After a short while, he broke clear of the trees, and immediately decided that it was not necessary to clamber any further up to the summit itself—he could see perfectly well from where he was. The sky above him was totally free of obstructions, while the trees below him blocked off the sight of any street lamps or other lights. He waited.

As the day began to border into night, he started to experience that same wonderful mood that comes with listening to a beautiful piece of music—the very finest of moments, yet at the same time the most transient of moments. He stood in quiet anticipation, getting himself ready for the coming performance in the skies above him. Surprisingly, there was nobody else about—was he the only person who wanted to come and enjoy the spectacle? Looking out from this particular vantage point he did seem to have the entire loch completely to himself.

The sky began to deepen into the most sumptuous shade of purplish blue, while beneath him the main islands of the loch stretched out in a darkening line that marked the position of the Highland Boundary Fault. The ground was too damp from days of persistent rain to allow him to sit down anywhere, so he decided to lean against a nearby wooden fence post to steady himself while he looked upwards at the slender silver moon and her attendant star, floating above him in the heavens. Each was wonderful in her own right—but *together* they were just stunning!

"Ah see, the loveliest of my sisters dance for us tonight. They know we are watching!" said a voice to his side.

Rab turned sharply, as he had not been aware of anybody approaching. A young man stood nearby, his face outlined in profile as he too looked skywards. With a chill, Rab knew that he had seen him before.

He paused, drew breath and then asked, "Is someone to die tonight? Is it me?"

"Why do you say that?"

"You are *death*, are you not?" said Rab, as calmly as he could muster.

"Ah, we have come to recognise one another on sight, have we not, Rab? And yet we don't seem to understand each other as well as we should. I am not *death*—I thought you might have realised that by now—but I can and do act as a *guide* for the dead, to the next world and back too sometimes."

"Then why you are here tonight, if not to prepare for someone's passing?" Rab asked, still more than a little worried.

"I come to Earth for many reasons, Rab, and not always to gather souls. Mine is a complex existence—I am here, and yet I am not here; I sit on the edge of the world's consciousness, on the boundaries twixt this and that; I am everywhere, and yet nowhere at the same time."

Then changing tack, he added, "You know, very few people seem able to see me, deeply absorbed as they usually are in their own little worlds—but you have been aware of me now and again, have you not?"

Rab didn't exactly feel that this was any kind of straight answer to a straight question—perhaps his visitor always talked in riddles like this—but he made his reply anyway.

"I don't think that I always see you when you are here—just *sometimes*. Why can I do that when others can't, and why not *all* of the time?" asked Rab remembering, in part at least, his previous sightings of the stranger.

The man drew in his breath and held it for some time. He seemed to be concentrating on something far away. Then, "Even I do not have all the answers, Rab. Some things are kept from me. One of the others has given you this gift of *sight*—probably my brother for some purpose best known to Himself. It will all become clear one day, I'm sure."

"So, will you not say why you have come tonight, then?" persisted Rab, gaining courage a little from the man's willingness to talk.

"For the same reasons as yourself, Rab—to watch, to admire, and quite simply to enjoy. Are they not beautiful to look at? I never tire of seeing them like this. I often like to come to share this wonderful sight with the living, even if they usually don't know that I'm there too!

Rab still felt that he was not being told the whole story. It all seemed a bit mysterious to him, but perhaps that was in the nature of his visitor's quicksilver personality.

His uninvited companion's tone became a little rueful. "Even to me, this world is full of puzzles and enigmas. I suppose I should be well accustomed by now to seeing what others see, while not being seen myself—but even after all this time, I find it just a little odd that most people don't seem to feel me there with them, not even a little bit. How can they be so blind?

"I have to say, though, that it's nice to have some company with me just once in a while, Rab—someone who can actually see me! Maybe I'm here to give you some reassurance, just to show you that it's OK to be a little more aware than other people, that it's alright to be different." This last bit was said with just a hint of a smile.

Rab ignored any hidden meaning in what had been said. "How often have you watched them like this?" he ventured, glancing upwards.

The man breathed softly and spoke in a near whisper. "Times without number, Rab, but I still look forward to each and every one of their appearances."

He turned to face Rab, who could see for the first time that he seemed to have a birthmark of some kind on his forehead, just visible in the evening light. It looked to be in the form of two outstretched wings. Then for a moment, he had that far-off look again as if he were listening to something that was both very distant and incredibly faint.

After a little time, the stranger seemed to remember where He was, and then looked very intently at Rab's face, his blue eyes burning. Momentarily Rab felt a point of coolness at the centre of his brow as if it had just been touched by a melting flake of snow. The sensation was not unpleasant, but it was *definitely* just a little strange.

"This should make things a little easier for you—the *Faerie Folk* will not trouble you now. I have spoken with them and they will keep their distance. Perhaps I should have dealt with them earlier.

"You will see me seven times in total in this life, Rab. More than that number would burn you out and destroy you utterly. You have now managed four sightings. As we move inexorably towards the final one, you will find yourself able to speak to me more fully and with better understanding, and I in turn will be able to answer you with greater ease. There is nothing to be afraid of—I am not here to hurt you."

Finally, Rab felt that he had his answer, even if he did not understand it particularly well. He sensed, however, that his visitor was about to depart. Curiosity, however, got the better of him about something that had been said earlier. Looking skywards again, he asked,

"You said that these were the *loveliest* of your sisters. Will the others not be jealous and seek their revenge on you? The legends are full of the anger of the Immortals when they feel slighted. There are so many stories about just how easy it is to offend them."

The man laughed heartily. "Oh yes, you can depend on it— *but they will have to catch me first!"*

He flashed a grin—and then vanished.

Chapter 11

Rab stayed watching the heavens above him for some time more—and yes, after the disappearance of his visitor it did still seem that some of His magic still remained. It was like the slow movement of some wonderful concerto that he had heard at the concert hall in Glasgow. The agonising beauty at the very heart of the piece would eventually come to an end, leaving only a memory of where it had touched the heart so tenderly. After the concert was over, and he was out on the street heading homewards, it had always been the slow movement that lingered in his mind, always that tune that played or sang inside his head.

Similarly, there was something from his recent encounter on Conic Hill that would not leave him. He ran it all through his mind and in time came to that momentary cool touch on his forehead. What was that all about, then? Was it some kind of anointing? Did it mean anything at all?

He shed a tear, not knowing why or for whom he wept. He felt drained and yet fulfilled at the same time. His recent conversation haunted him, and filled him somehow with a soft glow, though quite what it was a glow *of*, he couldn't say. There was a feeling of bitter-sweetness about it—not actually unpleasant, but slightly troubling nevertheless.

He descended the hill, taking care not to slip on the wet path in the darkness. There was a slight lump in his throat and he felt quite empty, transparent even. When he finally reached the spot where he had left his bike, he stopped to take one last look at the departing moon and her fair companion. Soon everything would be quite black, with only the faint light of the remaining stars to keep him company.

He walked his bike the few yards into Balmaha itself, stopping by the edge of the water for a little before leaving for home. He wondered why he suddenly felt so exhausted, as he was young and fit, and had done this run many times in the past without difficulty. Perhaps he was a little overwrought and wearied from his experience on Conic Hill?

He leant his arms on the handlebars and listened to the sounds of the night. A faint, ever so faint, sound of singing came to him across the water. It was one of the tricks of the loch, that even a whisper could travel a great distance over its surface. Others said that it was the sound of the Faerie, and to beware if you heard it! Just for an instant, the spot on his forehead burned cold with ice-fire.

After a few minutes, he felt strengthened and mounted his bike, making sure that his lights were set up correctly. He headed off. Under the trees that lined the road it was pitch black, yet despite the small size of the headlamp it still seemed incredibly bright as it cut into the darkness. For most of the way, there was nobody else on the road but when a car did come by, he turned away his head so that he would not be blinded by its powerful lights. For much of the time, however, the only sound was that of his own breathing and the swish of bicycle tyres on the surface of the road.

He didn't want to go home to the inevitable bedlam that he would find there, but he really had no choice. Balloch itself seemed deserted as he cycled through, and he saw no one anywhere on the streets. Pulling into the driveway of his house, he dismounted and headed for the shed where his bike was normally stored. He locked it away and then stopped. It was not yet particularly late in the evening, so he unlocked the shed door again and picked up his violin from where it had been hanging on its peg since his last practice. If anyone was particularly interested, they would know from the sound of the instrument that he had returned safely.

He didn't hear the music that he played—it seemed that someone else was using his fingers and that someone else apart from himself was doing the listening. He felt completely lost and abandoned in a far strange place, altogether shut away from this world—until he heard a soft knock on the door of the shed. His little sister looked up at him when he opened it and said with a slight catch in her voice.

"Oh, Rab, that music was so beautiful! I don't remember hearing it before. Was it something that you just made up, or did you learn it somewhere? Will you play it again?"

"Oh, I don't think I could find the notes a second time, little one," he said. "Did you really like it? Can you sing any of it for me?"

She concentrated for a little while, then shook her head. "I can't sing—you know that—and even if I could I don't think I would remember any of it. I just thought that it was lovely, though!"

They both laughed together and yet felt a little awkward too. Rab had never heard her talk of music before. Except for himself, the whole family was essentially tone deaf, and he was surprised at her words. He thought that maybe he had just been bowing aimlessly on the strings of his fiddle, and yet she claimed that she had been moved by the melody he had played. If she were just a little older, he would have thought she was making fun of him—or was practising her feminine guiles on a helpless male victim!

He locked up the shed and walked back with his sister to the house. She immediately joined the rest of the family to watch a noisy television programme, all thoughts of the music that she had just heard already lost to her. Rab retreated to his room and switched on the radio to listen to a concert on the BBC. He tried to read but found himself staring at the pages without taking in any of their content. Eventually, he gave up, and just listened to the music.

His mind returned once again to the meeting on Conic Hill. Something really rather special had happened, but he was not sure what it was—it lay just outside of his awareness. Perhaps it was better to leave it that way. Sometimes too much analysis had the opposite effect from the one intended, and the meaning became *less* clear with study, *more* difficult to grasp.

Time for sleep, he thought.

Chapter 12

Rab saw through his college training in Glasgow as he had planned, commuting into the city every weekday on the train. He was able to use his new student travel pass, which effectively gave him an unlimited number of trips on the Balloch/Glasgow route. It proved useful too when he wanted to get to the city's excellent libraries on Saturdays, or even to a concert some other time at weekends.

His student grant was adequate, but not overly generous. Any extras he paid for himself, from his earnings in Balloch. Just as long as he was not extravagant in his spending, he could get through the academic year without slipping into the red or having to ask for money from anyone to help him out. His family offered no help to him, and he knew better than to ask.

It was perhaps just as well that he had a quiet nature and that he enjoyed private pleasures rather than the usual extrovert pursuits of the young. He had no spare cash for boozy nights out—which he would not have enjoyed anyway—but instead he took advantage of pretty well anything going culturally that was either free or cost very little. There was always something on somewhere that he could go to if he found himself at a loose end. Not everything available was of the highest international standard—inevitably—but it did get him out and about and opened his eyes to the wider world of art and music.

He began to get known and recognised on the culture circuit, and in time people would approach him and stop briefly for a chat. Usually, they were very well dressed, no doubt with fancy professional jobs and big houses. Sometimes they were academics, teaching perhaps at the university. He was cautious with all of them, as he felt that their friendship, if that was what it was, might cost him money that he did not have. He could not afford the same expensive seats in the concert hall or stop for a designer coffee during the performance interval, and he had to choose what he could or could not attend according to the ticket price—he certainly did not dress as well, either! He thought it prudent to keep a polite distance between them.

In fact, they understood his circumstances very well. They could see from his simple and unassuming attire that he did not have much money. He was always washed and scrubbed, however, so quite clearly he took care of himself and took pride in the little that he had. That he was always on his own told them he had a strong personality and was not afraid to pursue his cultural interests even if he could not necessarily find anyone else to share these with. When spoken to, he was always polite and could give an educated response to any comments they made about the particular exhibition or musical performance he was attending. They noted, however, that he never bought a programme—too expensive—so his evident understanding of the work in question must come from elsewhere. He had been spotted more than once in the Mitchell Library on Saturdays, and they guessed correctly that he would familiarise himself there with any background material that seemed necessary to him. He therefore didn't need a programme, except for details of the performers—and information about *them* was usually pinned up in the foyer.

He still missed Anja. Even if she did not share all of his interests, she had always been a good listener when he talked about what he had been listening to or seeing. Her comments were often very much to the point, and he would ask himself afterwards why he had not thought of it himself. He hoped that she was OK. He wondered if she remembered him.

In those days, Sundays in the west of Scotland were deadly. Nothing much was open, and paradoxically if it was your only day off in the week, there was practically nothing enjoyable for you to do. Rab usually reserved the day for college work, and before going round to take Smozo out for his daily exercise, he would stay in his room and catch up with his studies. He had no interest in church and did not much care for those people who did.

To Rab's surprise, he was approached by an eminent doctor and his wife at one Saturday night concert—he had seen them several times before and they had become nodding acquaintances. They were having some friends around for

Sunday lunch the following week, and would Rab care to join them? He accepted graciously and then began to worry about the implications. With his student pass, his train fare into Glasgow was not a problem but he had nothing smart to wear, and was it not customary to turn up with a little present of some kind? What was he to do? He made the best use of existing resources, that's what he did.

At the appointed hour on the Sunday in question, Rab rang the bell at the front door of a beautiful grand house in the posh West End of Glasgow. It was the doctor's wife—who insisted on being called by her first name, Lisbet—who answered.

"Come in, Rab, I'm so glad that you could make it. Some of the others are here already, but one or two are running just a little bit late."

Rab entered and offered a little package that he was carrying.

"I wanted to bring you some flowers, but they are impossible to find in the shops in Balloch during the winter. My young sister made this little paper and silk posy, and wondered if you would like it to help cheer you up in the run-up to the shortest day. She put a drop of attar of roses on it to help with the illusion that it's real."

Now, in the rather stiff social circles which were her normal social environment, spontaneous little gestures of this kind were rare. Lisbet felt a momentary lump in her throat, but with the kindest of smiles she took Rab's coat and ushered him towards the living room.

Over a pair of plain black trousers, he wore a snow-white shirt and a borrowed waistcoat, into which he had tucked the rolled gold watch chain that Granda had left him. There was no pocket watch to go with it, but Rab intended correcting that just as soon as he had a little money to spare. He looked smart.

Regaining her composure, Lisbet said, "Thank you, Rab. That was very sweet of you—you really are the perfect gentleman. Please thank your sister for me. What's her name again?"

Rab entered the enormous living room. Various people were seated around on the beautiful antique furniture, sipping aperitifs and chatting—a bit pretentiously, Rab thought—about last night's symphony concert. Nobody as much as looked in his direction. They were far too busy being perfect to acknowledge someone like himself.

He was offered a drink, and asked for a tonic water—he didn't drink alcohol anyway, and he found the bitter taste of the tonic stimulating on the tongue before eating. He sat quietly, casually taking in the beautiful paintings and lovely silk rugs without seeming overly curious about them. He totally ignored those who were ignoring *him* and made no attempt to speak to anyone.

Suddenly, there was a commotion at the front door. Lisbet went to attend to it, and after a few moments, the great international soprano *Angélique de la Victoire* swept into the room, accompanied by her husband. Rab was gobsmacked, as she had been the performer at the previous night's concert, singing Ravel's *Shéherazade* and then *Dido's Lament* by Purcell. The Ravel had been just exquisite, and not for nothing did they say that she sang it better than anyone else alive.

Unfortunately, her English was heavily accented—to put it mildly—and when she switched to that language for *Dido's Lament* her rendering of the work was, well, lamentable! She had only agreed to perform it as somebody had convinced her that it would please an English-speaking audience.

Quite quickly now, they all moved through to the dining room and seated themselves at the table.

In this erudite company, Rab hoped and prayed that he would not be asked to comment on last night's concert, but of course, that is exactly what some stuck-up young woman did, hoping to disadvantage this upstart low-class visitor in front of everyone. She had seen him turn up at the door in a *duffel* coat, of all things, and decided to teach him his place—if he didn't know it already!

"And what did you think of last night's performance, eh, *Rab* is it?" saying his name as if it were difficult to pronounce. She hoped to catch him off guard—or even better, out of his depth.

Rab answered that he had never heard the Ravel so beautifully sung, and until the previous evening he had not been aware of the subtlety of expression that existed in that particular composer's writing. He hoped that was going to be it. He absolutely didn't want to be drawn on the Purcell! Some chance!

Angélique positively purred with delight at his comments about her singing of Shéherazade. Then they got to it. "Deed you enjoy mey Dido?" she asked, apparently unaware of just how awful her singing of English actually was.

Rab was cornered.

"*Je préfère 'Les Troyens à Carthage', madame. Je crois que Berlioz comprend mieux que Purcell l'agonie de cette reine torturée. Est-ce que vous chantez cette Didon?*"

There was a surprised silence around the table. Nobody had expected a response of this sort—and certainly not in French.

"*Jeune home,*" she said after a pause, "*je crois que vous avez raison, mais il faut répondre 'non'. Je voudrais la chanter, mais j'en ai peur—je crains pour la voix. Dites-moi, vous chantez, hein?*"

"*Comme un corbeau, madame, mais j'ai un violon quand je veux jouer de la musique.*"

[*translation:* "I prefer Dido in the 'Trojans in Carthage', madame. I think that Berlioz understands better than Purcell the agony of this tortured queen. Do you sing that particular Dido?"

"Young man, I think you're right. I would like to sing it, but I'm afraid of it—I fear for my voice. Tell me, do *you* sing?"

"Like a crow, madame, but I have a violin when I want to make music."]

Rather quickly, Angelique had become enchanted with this quiet and delightfully unassuming Scottish boy who could handle himself intelligently in her own language. Reverting to what she imagined was standard English for the benefit of all at the table, she said, "Pleeze, play for us *après le déjeuner.* Eef you do zis, I sing a leetle too!"

With great gusto she then launched into an account of her latest adventures with this or that famous conductor, moving without warning from one language to another then back again. Performer that she was, she played outrageously on her apparent lack of understanding of proper English—it was extremely difficult not to laugh out loud as her stories got taller and taller.

Rab was the first to see that she was taking them all for a ride, and eventually he guffawed loudly at a scabrous comment she made about the president of France, knowing that it was hopelessly untrue. She burst into laughter herself, having wondered just how far she could get before someone twigged that she was making it all up. Lisbet, who had no French, had been struggling to follow the dialogue with Rab and smiled painfully politely at jokes she could not hope to understand. She was pleased, however, that at least *someone* seemed to have the measure of her irrepressible guest!

They ate extremely well, and afterwards at coffee back in the living room, Angélique beckoned imperiously to Rab and demanded that he play. A violin was fetched from a cupboard and he stepped out into the hallway to tune it, out of the hearing of the guests. Kept somewhere on a forgotten shelf it might have been, but it was still a much finer instrument than any he had previously played—and that certainly included his own that he kept at home in Balloch.

While he tuned the violin, he considered just what he should play. Everybody at lunch that day had been to concert after concert in the city, and at one time or another had heard the very greatest players perform there. He thought it best to avoid unfortunate comparisons, and so he chose two pieces by the French composer Rameau. They were fine works—yes—but relatively unknown, so the chances were that nobody present at lunch that day would be familiar with them or would judge him unkindly against the standards of others playing the same music.

He came back into the living room, where everyone was now enjoying their coffee—and even the occasional liqueur for those not driving—and stood poised and ready to play. He waited.

The stuck-up little madam who earlier had tried to place Rab at a disadvantage was seated on a chaise longue, cornering some poor Professor of Classics who had been careless enough not to see her coming. She was seriously annoyed at being upstaged by this young *peasant*—as she saw it—at the lunch table, and was doing her best to extract her revenge. In a loud shrill voice, she was boring the poor academic—and everyone else in the room—to death with some utterly pointless story about her childhood and upbringing in a country estate in Perthshire. Everyone wondered how long it would take for her to finish.

Now, Angélique may have sung for kings, queens, presidents—and even the pope on one occasion—and justifiably had a reputation as the finest singer of *chansons* on the planet, but through her grandmother she had the blood of generations of fishwives flowing through her veins. She knew when positive action was called for, and she knew how to deliver it. She rose from her seat and stomped over to the young woman, who was still talking about nothing in particular to nobody in particular—just as long as she could loudly attract attention to herself.

"Shut ze trap!" said Angélique fiercely. "Eef you find zis deeficult, I 'elp you."

The diva then floated—yes, that was the word—like a Grand Duchess back over to her seat, and with the sweetest of smiles and a gentle nod to the other guests, sank magnificently into the plush upholstery of her chair.

Rab suppressed a grin, and with a slight inclination of his head in her direction, picked up the violin and played the two pieces he had selected. They were a good choice for the acoustic of this lovely room and a good choice for the calibre of guest, who received the music exactly as he had intended. There was a little ripple of applause. With another graceful bow of the head, Rab raised the violin to his chin once more.

He next played a lilting Hebridean melody, one that soared and swooped like a graceful white bird of the sea—it was a tune that Anja had loved. It told of wild places, and of things found there that were familiar—and yet somehow beyond reach, too. It carried with it the scent of windswept shores and of damp silent mists that cleared only gradually under the pale warmth of the sun. It told of heartbreak and of joy. It spoke of everything, and yet of nothing.

When he got to the end and had again acknowledged his applause, he placed the violin down on top of the Bechstein grand piano in the corner of the room to indicate that he had finished. So moved was she, Angélique actually wept when she heard the last piece he played, at one point holding a delicate handkerchief to her eyes. She sat silently—something that was unusual in her—and drew her thoughts down deep inside herself, to where her soul dwelt. After a little while, she gathered herself together and said, "Now I seeng. *Mon cher!*"

This last was directed at her husband, who came over to the piano and played for her as she sang a medley of her favourite songs. Of course, she was just exquisite—and great fun too! Mercifully she did not attempt to sing anything in English, though.

When the little cameo performances were over, they all settled down again for some more coffee. Rab, however, slipped quietly over to an alcove containing a life-size marble bust that he had noticed earlier but had not yet had a chance to examine closely. It was the head of a very beautiful young man, wearing a cap with two wings sprouting from the sides. He was mesmerised by it.

"They usually call Him *the Messenger of the Gods*, but that is to diminish Him, I think." The classics Professor was standing by his side, enjoying Rab's fascination with the sculpted head before him.

"He is a great god in his own right; the God of philosophy, of commerce, of boundaries of all kinds—and most importantly for *us,* He has the reputation of caring for humanity and is the God who accompanies the souls of the dead to the next plane to ensure their safe passage. He is the only Olympian who can travel freely between different worlds, different states of existence—the others do so only rarely and with difficulty. He is also the metasexual god."

Rab was not quite sure what that last bit meant, but he didn't let it trouble him. He noted, however, that the professor used the present tense when he talked as if he were not speaking of some stone-cold deity from ancient times, but of someone alive and with us still.

"Do people ever see Him? How did this sculptor know what He looked like?" Rab asked.

"Aha! Those who see Him do not often talk about it, in case they're thought mad. He does have a reputation for adopting many disguises, although He is always beautiful no matter how He might otherwise appear—even when He takes the likeness of a beggar or a very old man. Like all of the immortals, He is to be treated with respect—and dare I say, caution."

"Why is that?" said Rab. "Is He dangerous?"

"Let's just say that He and His kind have their own agendas, and these do not always coincide with our own. He has a reputation for playing tricks too!"

There was a gale of laughter from the other end of the room as Angélique delivered another of her wicked little stories. Whether you believed any of them or not was quite irrelevant— they were always enormous fun!

Much though he was enjoying the afternoon, Rab was beginning to worry about the time. He decided that he should take his leave and head for home. He still had things to do before lectures the next morning.

With exquisite courtesy, he thanked his hosts for the wonderful lunch and commented how privileged he felt to have had the opportunity to get to know the assembled guests a little better. The toffee-nosed young woman glared at him.

Angelique demanded a little kiss on the cheek before he departed, saying, *"Au revoir, mon enfant. Souviens-toi d'Angélique de la Victoire!"*

Without further ceremony, he left and walked to the railway station for his train.

Chapter 13

At last, the day came for Rab's graduation. His mother and sister came for the ceremony—his father was far too busy doing something else to be bothered attending. In the huge hall of the College, the students all lined up in an orderly fashion and one by one went through the ritual of being capped and given their diplomas. The whole affair was dealt with extremely efficiently, and in no time at all, they were all back out in the street wondering what to do next.

Rab decided that they should celebrate by going for a cream tea somewhere, but they had to walk away some distance to get clear of everyone else trying to do something of the same sort. Eventually, they found a nice little teashop and settled in. They gorged themselves on the delicious freshly baked scones—still warm from the oven—topped with cream and homemade raspberry jam. Was this Scotland's greatest contribution to world cuisine? Even if it was not, they all felt at that particular moment that it must come close!

When all was done, they separated to go their different ways. Mother and daughter sped to the shops, while Rab went to the offices of the company who had interviewed him for a job just a couple of weeks before. They had wanted to inspect his paper qualifications before formalising his appointment, and his new diploma would do the trick perfectly. Rab now had only another two weeks before he began his new life as a paid employee, and he relished the opportunity for a little time off after all his exertions during the run-up to the final exams only a short while before.

Rab himself did a little special shopping and took the train back to Balloch. From the station, he went straight to Sara's house and asked if he could come in, even if it was a little early for Smozo's usual daily outing. Sara was slightly surprised to see him so soon, but she welcomed him warmly. She was excited by his graduation and wanted to hear every detail of the ceremony and how it had been carried out. At the sight of Rab, Smozo—who knew nothing of graduations—was merely excited!

Sara disappeared into the kitchen to make a pot of tea, and Rab placed a little cardboard box that he had brought with him on top of the coffee table. Sara returned with the tea and immediately spotted the box.

"I fetched a wee something for you and Smozo to help celebrate with me if you will," he said, opening up the little parcel as she poured out two cups of steaming tea. Inside was a *very* fancy cupcake, capped with icing and a glacé cherry. "I've already stuffed myself with a cream scone, so I'll have only a tiny bit to keep you company. We'll probably have to force-feed poor Smozo with his share. You know how reticent he is with anything sweet!"

She laughed, and carefully cut the cake into portions so that individually they could take as much or as little as they wanted. The very last piece went into the dog—effortlessly!

"Now, tell me how they carried out the capping ceremony. Things change, you know, and I wonder if they do it the same way nowadays as in my own time."

Later, when walking out in the fields above the town with Smozo, Rab considered how best to use the little rest time that he had before starting work. He was bone-tired after his final year studying, and needed to get out and about in the fresh air as much as possible in order to recover. He had no money to go away anywhere, so he decided to spend time walking in the hills around the loch, sometimes with Smozo and sometimes not, depending on the distances involved. There were various public footpaths and walkways that criss-crossed the area and the exercise would do him a world of good. He would take the opportunity to consider his future plans, where he wanted to live, and how he thought that his life might pan out.

He now had a job in the city and an income in the offing. He wondered just a little whether he wanted to move permanently into town, close to his work, but on balance decided that Balloch suited him admirably for the time being. Besides, Smozo still had a few years left in him and by now Rab was far too fond of the dog to abandon him to fate. Also, Sara was clearly ailing and he felt that he needed to be there for them both—he owed them that for their friendship to him in recent years.

He didn't want to stay with his family any longer, though. They were indifferent, even hostile sometimes, to everything that he stood for. He wondered what it might be like to live somewhere with *music* as a background, rather than the din of constant squabbling—bliss probably! It was time for him to move on.

He had not yet had the opportunity to build up any financial resources, so finding the deposit on the purchase of a house was out of the question for the time being. He wondered if he could arrange the rental of a small flat somewhere in the area, and decided to put out feelers over the coming fortnight while he still had some free time. He was known to be quiet and decent, and in a smallish community like Balloch, this could count for a lot. He would not need much, and with luck, he could find somewhere suitable either in Balloch itself or in its near vicinity.

Rab started his search almost immediately, and to his surprise found what he was looking for quite quickly. There was a series of grand houses in the area, and one, in particular, had a separate coach house with some living accommodation above. It didn't amount to much, but it was warm and dry and within easy walking distance of the town itself. The owners were only too happy to rent it to him, as they knew of his solid reputation in the area and were glad to have someone they could trust close to the house—somebody who would not bring with him any noisy friends, or have late-night parties.

His family made no offers of help with finding his first advance instalment on the rent, but without being asked Sara stepped in to lend him the money.

"This is what friends are for," she said. "We help each other in various ways—and besides, both Smozo and myself would like to have you nearby. Shall we say that you can pay me back within the twelvemonth? Good, that's it settled then!"

The mews flat was tiny, and the meagre furniture that it contained was barely adequate for his needs. The rent was more than reasonable, though, and Rab could see for himself how with only a small financial outlay he could adapt everything to suit his requirements. There was even an honoured place for his violin, too!

In no time at all, he was settled in and enjoying his freedom from studies on the one hand, and from domestic conflict on the other. Perhaps inevitably, there was a standoff with his father who could not miss the opportunity to be snide about Rab's new home.

"All those years of study, Rab, and all those books! It's not much to show for your efforts, is it—but then, I always had you marked as a loser!"

"It's a new beginning," Rab replied, "and an end to things that I don't want or need. I can grow from here, in ways that are beyond your understanding. Mine is a world of increasing awareness; yours is one of no awareness at all. You have never taken any pride in what I am or do, or shown any interest in me as a human being over the years, so what would you know about my aspirations in life?"

Rab warmed to his theme. "It wouldn't have taken much for you even to acknowledge my existence from time to time, but you did not. In your limited way of thinking, it probably struck you as being clever in some kind of way. Just remember that one day you may be dependent on *my* goodwill, as you grow old and slip into your dotage. Pray to whatever god you believe in that I am more generous with my help than you have been with yours."

They never spoke to each other again. Nothing was missed on either side.

Chapter 14

Rab's first winter in the mews flat passed uneventfully, and he soon felt quite comfortable and secure in his new home. For the first time in his life, he had an income that he could start to enjoy, with spare time that was not taken up by constant studying. He wasn't really used to either money or leisure time, of course, and he reckoned it was going to take him some time to adjust to any new regime.

Old habits die hard, do they not? He had always been the kind that liked to be learning something or another, to be extending himself in some way, and he decided that in life he would always take classes of some sort, even if the subject itself seemed quite trivial to others. He found a basic evening course in cookery, one that he could attend after work, and began to experiment with tackling something a little more interesting than merely opening tin cans or boiling pre-cooked dinners. It was all a bit new, and he found it fun.

Rab's younger sister Ellie, of whom he was rather fond, began to pop around regularly with her new boyfriend Tam. She was coming up for sixteen years old and getting ready to leave school—her *beau* was one year older and had already made his transition into the adult world. Neither one of them had any academic pretensions whatsoever, and consequently had no desire to follow Rab's career path—a job was quite simply a job that earned money to live on. They were altogether quite happy with that idea.

Rab suspected that they would actually marry soon—you could do so legally at the age of sixteen in Scotland—following the time-honoured practice of escaping one family nest by setting up another one! He hoped that they wouldn't rush into it and perhaps take a little time before making their move, but he would understand perfectly well if they decided earlier rather than later to escape the claustrophobic atmosphere of both of their present homes. *They would make good parents one day too*, he thought.

With his new cookery skills (!) he was able to feed them well when they came around, and Tam hinted to Ellie that she might like to go on the same evening course. She practically battered him, as she was very proud of her own abilities in that direction—she had done classes in cookery at school—but in truth, there had been little opportunity elsewhere to show off what she had learnt. Cooking at both of their family homes was extremely basic and predictable, and you could tell what day of the week it was by the menu for the evening meal—and did vegetables really have to be boiled to death and beyond before they were slopped onto the plate?

Rab suggested that they could come around once each week and prepare whatever meal they wished for the three of them to eat. He only had a Baby Belling to cook on (a sturdy and reliable mini cooker, with two electric hotplates and a basic oven) but it was surprising what you could do with it.

Ellie jumped at the chance. Rab provided the money for the ingredients, and Ellie did the shopping. A few utensils and cooking pots followed, and before long they were experimenting with dishes that had been unknown to them up to that time. Occasionally, Rab would buy sweet peppers or aubergines in a Glasgow delicatessen before coming home after work (these were rarities in Scottish shops in those days, and absolutely non-existent in Balloch), and they would try out different ways of preparing them. In turn, Ellie became interested in local farm produce and sought out fresh parsnips and turnips while the winter lasted, and spring crops when the weather improved. They all loved it, and Rab's new home rang to the sound of their laughter and good humour.

When he felt sufficiently confident in his abilities, Rab invited Sara—and Smozo of course—around for a meal. She was weaker these days and arrived by taxi where once she would have been happy to walk. The dog dashed around, intensely curious about Rab's new home—full of his friend's belongings and attendant scents—but he eventually settled down on the threadbare carpet to wait for his own meal.

Sara smiled quietly. No need to worry, she told herself, everything will be alright. That mince pie that Rab had made especially for her was quite delicious and he had got the pastry just right. She particularly liked the way that the potatoes had not been peeled and boiled stupid in the customary Scottish manner, but were simply washed, steamed and served up while still in their skins—with just a little dash of melting butter over the top. Quite wonderful! *Rab might never become a cordon bleu chef,* she thought, *but you would always eat well in his house*!

She suspected, though, that the dessert had been prepared as much with Smozo in mind as herself, and her smile broadened as the dog consumed his share with a grunt of uncontrolled delight. He'll be happy here when the time comes and won't want for anything. They would both be just fine.

The year had now swung back into the warmer months when it was possible to spend more time out of doors. Rab still helped out when he could in the harbour, more because he enjoyed it than for any financial gain. Mucking about on boats—sailing them even, sometimes—was one of those wonderfully simple pleasures that could not be explained to anyone who was not an aficionado of such deep spiritual matters. He wondered what particular branch of theology covered such weighty issues— well, not really, he didn't!

By the middle of May, the weather had become blissfully clear and warm, but without the sultriness that could come in later summer months. Balloch sprang to life as tourists from nearby Glasgow and beyond clamoured for their little bit of countryside, descending on the harbour area for ice creams, sun hats and all the rest of the usual paraphernalia of a day out.

Rab loved the clatter of all the activity and laughed inwardly at the antics of happy children splashing around in the shallows of the fresh clear water of the loch. Not everyone could afford a boat of their own—not by a long chalk—but it was a characteristic of holidaying spots all over the world that even a simple day-tripper could feel ownership and a sense of involvement in the movement of small craft when passing into and out of harbour.

For a moment, Rab remembered his Granda and their days together looking out for steamers arriving in Rothesay, full of passengers escaping from the grimmer reality of Glasgow's heavy industry and cramped housing. These were his earliest memories and he treasured them, at the same time wondering just a little how his upbringing might have been easier had the old man survived to help him through the difficult times.

In fact, these simple recollections had indeed strengthened him over the years. Granda had been the very first person he knew who had believed in him, who had given Rab a sense of who he was and what he could become. The boy might have been very young when he learnt these things, but that stiffening of the backbone and the nascent awareness of himself had never left him. Small beginnings perhaps, but even the mightiest tree grows from the tiniest of seeds.

That distant holiday in Rothesay was still occupying his thoughts when he practically ran into a man eating some kind of iced confection on the pavement outside the village store where he had obviously just acquired it. He was dressed garishly —why did people always have to wear silly clothes when the sun came out? Rab's attention was immediately caught, however, by a vulgar pair of sunglasses fashioned like birds' wings.

"Not my usual impeccable sartorial style, eh Rab? I like to have my fun sometimes, too, you know."

Rab stood dumbstruck. There was no doubt who this was, but his mind raced as to why He was there. In a flash, he saw the reason.

"It's Sara, isn't it?" he said, "but I think that You're here early. It hasn't happened yet, has it? I always seem to see You just before the actual event."

The man nodded approvingly. "You're getting quite good at this, Rab. Soon, you will not even need me as a trigger but will see quite clearly for yourself. This is all for the better.

"Come! There is still time. Smozo is holding the fort for us, but he's getting concerned as he knows that something is wrong."

They walked swiftly through the town, unseen be anybody that they passed, even by those whom Rab could count as acquaintances and friends. He knew that his companion had once commented that He was usually unobserved by those around Him, but Rab had been unaware that this might on occasion apply to himself as well. They seemed to cover the ground more swiftly than seemed quite natural too, but Rab didn't care. He was worried.

"When we arrive, will she be able to see You as well?" he asked.

"I am there already, although in another guise. She is perfectly aware of my presence."

Rab let that one go. It didn't really surprise him that his visitor could be in two places at once—more actually—but he would need time to think about it all carefully later.

Soon, they arrived at Sara's house to find her sitting in the garden, apparently enjoying the warm sunshine. Spent blossom from the ornamental hawthorn tree was gently falling down to carpet the lawn by her side in a semblance of winter snow. Smozo was with her, his chin resting on her knee as he looked up into her face. She looked a little distracted, wearied even, but did not appear to be in any pain. A smile formed on her face as she caught sight of Rab.

"You too, my dear! I think that we are all ready, then." She inclined her head in a graceful nod and as a faint shadow crossed over her eyes she sweetly departed this life, just another little white flower drifting away on the warm breath of a gentle spring breeze.

Chapter 15

Sara had asked that she be cremated. Her ashes were to be taken out to the hills overlooking the loch, to a favourite spot from her childhood and one that was well known to her sister. Jenny showed a remarkable calmness and self-control at the funeral ceremony in the crematorium, but Rab knew that she would disintegrate at some point later. He stayed close to her at the customary reception later in a local hotel, after the service and the committal. She managed to smile a little and to speak to everyone who was there, but her heart was breaking.

"I'm so glad that you are here," she said. "Everyone is looking to me for strength today, but I am in need of it myself. Will you come back with me to Sara's house while we start to think about what to do with everything?"

Later, when they were seated in Sara's living room, Rab said, "What about Smozo? He's not mine, you know, although he's staying with me at the moment. I suppose, though, that he didn't officially belong to Sara either. He's had quite a chequered history."

"I've worried a bit about it too," she replied. "What's for the best, do you think?"

"He's very welcome to live with me permanently," he said. "He's just a bit unsettled yet, as you might expect, but he's a resilient little blighter, and he'll pull through just fine, I think."

Smozo's fate was thus sealed! He missed Sara terribly, as dogs do when their owners die, but he compensated by focussing totally on Rab. He quickly got used to Rab's daily work schedule—but was never happier than when the weekend came around and they could spend more time together.

During the working week, the dog always got a good run early in the morning when Rab got up, and another one when he returned from the office. Smozo adopted the routine of snoozing during the day, patiently waiting for the return of his pal through the door and then greeting him with an explosion of wet nose and frantic tail. The free days were still special, though! He liked to stay close to Rab as they went about their shopping in the town and he made his own friends with shopkeepers and local worthies, who always hailed him with a kind word or two. Rab did his best to keep him busy and well exercised. They enjoyed their time in each other's company as if they both knew that it could not last forever.

Jenny occupied herself with clearing out Sara's house. Her two adult daughters came to help, so there was really nothing much for Rab to do there. When the time came, though, Jenny asked him to come with her while she dealt with the ashes. Her daughters backed off that one!

They drove in Jenny's car to a small parking lot partway up the loch. There was no footpath, but they climbed easily through the trees to a clearing about one hundred yards or so up the hillside, Rab carrying Sara in a small wooden casket. It was a lovely spot, one of the thousands around the shores of this inland sea where wonderful views could be had of the hills and the water, and where time seemed to stand still for an eternity or two.

Jenny couldn't cope any longer, as memories of earlier days playing here with her sister came flooding back. She broke down at last, in no fit state to make any decisions about how to deal with Sara's remains. Rab realised that it was up to himself to sort it out.

The casket was a simple wooden affair but made of good pitch pine from a recycled church pew. Nobody had said what was to be done with the container later, and given the durability of the timber, it quite clearly would not disintegrate easily by itself. He didn't suppose that anyone else would ever want to use it again—and Jenny certainly wouldn't wish to keep it! It just didn't seem right to discard it either.

He took up some sticks from fallen branches and dug into the soft peat of the hillside to make a shallow recess about a foot or so deep. He paused before placing the little box in its grave and asked Jenny if it was OK to do it this way. She recovered sufficiently to nod her approval—the part she had dreaded the most had been scattering Sara's ashes out over the hillside. This was better.

Rab returned a few days later on his bicycle, carrying in his knapsack a tiny wooden cross he had bought from one of the church shops in Glasgow. The disturbed soil where they had placed Sara would settle soon and become overgrown once more, and it seemed prudent to mark the spot for future reference. He had brought a flower from Sara's garden with him too, and he laid it gently over her. Quietly, he bade her farewell.

In truth, he was the only person who ever came there again—Jenny could never face it.

***

A few years later, the inevitable happened. When she heard the news, Jenny came over and drove Rab back to the car park by the roadside near where they had once laid Sara's ashes in the ground. This time Rab carried a spade and a small heavy bundle in a bag up the hillside. Jenny point blank refused to come with him. She sat in the car by the water's edge and waited for his return.

He dug a pit close by Sara and laid Smozo to his rest. They had never been able to put an age on him but the vet was of the opinion that he had actually lived his full span, and that it was cruel to keep him alive when everything was beginning to fail. Somewhere in their many chats together, Rab had promised the dog that when the time came he would not let him suffer but would deal with it as gently as he could. He had kept to his word.

He was better prepared than before and fixed a small marker, the kind that is used by gardeners to show where they had planted seeds, by the graveside. It simply gave the dog's name and the date he had died. He then took a few heavy stones he found nearby and laid them over the disturbed soil, in order to discourage foxes. In time, he would come back and remove them so that there would be as little trace of the burial as possible. Apart from himself, nobody would ever be able to find the two friends and intrude upon their peace.

When he returned to the car park, Jenny said that they could both do with a cup of tea somewhere, and suggested that they headed up the loch to the village of Tarbet and the hotel there. On the way, she asked,

"Was *He* there, like before?"

Rab considered the question for a little while before answering. "I didn't see Him this time, but I *felt* Him quite strongly, watching and noting what was happening. I am rationed as to how many times I am allowed get a sighting, and it must be that my remaining two viewings are important for me and needed at another time."

Jenny commented, in her soft lilting way, "You have come a long way since we first talked about this, Rab, and your understanding of these things has grown considerably. You will never be a fairground clairvoyant—as I am sometimes thought to be—and I suspect that much of what others with the 'talent' can see is in actual fact hidden from *you*. Yours is a different ability and a much rarer thing. It must be a burden sometimes. Please remember that I am always there to listen to you if it gets too much. I can understand only up to a point, of course, but that's better than not being able to understand at all, is it not?"

They stopped for their afternoon tea and talked of other things.

Chapter 16

Rab was at something of a loss after Smozo died. People said that he should get another dog, but somehow he felt that this would be a betrayal of loyalty towards his old friend—though perhaps later at another time? On the other hand, perhaps not. It seemed odd, but he felt in his heart that Smozo was always with him, still keeping him company—still there, a part of him even.

Rab was not extravagant in his lifestyle, and his income had now increased to the point where he had a small surplus of funds, this time to be used for something other than the mere basics needed for survival. After discussion with his cronies at the harbour, he decided that he would build a small sailing boat—nothing too big or elaborate, but a capable little craft that would let him explore the islands of the loch.

He ordered some plans through a yachting magazine and set about acquiring the necessary materials. He had chosen the size and design of the boat carefully so that it could be built in the disused stable under his flat. Some tools he would need to buy; others he could borrow as they were needed.

He selected an American design which was popular at the time, a *Great Pelican,* specifically tailored for the amateur builder. Sixteen feet in length, it had enough covered accommodation to allow overnight stops—or even a weekend and longer if there was only one person. Importantly, it had a good reputation for seaworthiness, essential on this loch that could be so temperamental in its mood.

The boat was square ended and of shoal draft, but had a *drop keel* which when lowered enabled the craft to sail safely in deeper waters where conditions could become adverse. At the same time, the flat bottom allowed the craft to creep closer to land when the keel was raised. All of the islands on Loch Lomond were owned by somebody or other, and it was not always considered polite to camp on them at will. However, a shallow-draft vessel which drew only a few inches of water could be drawn up right up to their shores and moored comfortably, perhaps with her bow just resting on the beach. Nobody would be able to complain just as long as there was no mess or disturbance of any kind left behind.

Rab was by now quite an experienced sailor, and he had clear ideas on just how his craft was to be equipped and fitted out. He wanted everything to be simple, yet efficient and fit for purpose. He had never in his life been much accustomed to luxuries of any kind and he did not seek them in his boat. A chemical toilet and a tiny galley opposite his sleeping berth were practically his only concessions to modern civilised comforts.

Tam—and by extension, Ellie—became interested in the project, and came around whenever possible to help out. Rab was grateful for their input, and they, in turn, were happy to have somewhere to spend time together that was away from their respective suffocating home environments—and in a meeting place that did not cost them anything! Rab found that it was just as easy to feed three people as it was to cook for one if everyone pulled together just a little bit. In time, their simple meals together at the end of a working day became something of an anchor point in their young lives and helped them to bond together as a team.

It really didn't take much more than one winter to complete the boat, and the only factor which threatened to slow them down was Rab's cash flow—buying new equipment and materials from orthodox sources could be so expensive! His contacts at the harbour, however, alerted him to anything second-hand that was available, and with a little tender loving care, many otherwise discarded components were repaired and cleaned up for re-use—and at minimal cost.

One day, all was ready, and the boat was trailered to the lochside to be launched. Ellie was invited to perform the naming ceremony. With a grand flourish of her arms and an exaggerated air of solemnity, she splashed the contents of a small bottle of ginger ale over the bow and declared,

"I name this wee boatie *Snowdrop 2*, and wish safety and happiness to all who sail in her!"

The name would come as no surprise to anyone who knew of Rab's early life—and yet, apart from himself who could still remember it? The hull was a good strong shade of green in colour, her sails as white as snow. Bonny and trim, she still smelled of fresh paint and elbow grease!

The very next day, Rab took her out on her maiden voyage. As he explored her capabilities, he congratulated himself on the wisdom of his choice of design. She moved well through the water and cut neatly through currents and waves. When rain threatened, he could moor in the lee of some small island or headland, and shelter in the neat and cosy cabin.

With his *second-sighted* weather eye, he hoped to be able to avoid squalls and sudden showers. He had no wish to get caught out in the middle of the water if things turned bad. Proud though he was of *Snowdrop 2*, there was no point in tempting fate by ignoring the forces of nature. He was not an incautious person and was only too aware of what this beautiful yet treacherous loch could do to the unwary.

In the weeks to come, Rab took the boat out as often as he could, accompanied by Tam and Ellie whenever all three of them were free at the same time. They would tie up or drop anchor in one or other of the countless coves to be found around the loch and its islands, cooking their meals in the simple but efficient galley. They shared both the sailing and the food preparation, and Rab took pleasure in watching his sister and her boyfriend work seamlessly together—quietly understanding each other's thoughts and movements. *In their journey through life, they would be perfect for each other*, he thought.

Sometimes at weekends, if he had the chance to sail alone, he would disappear for a day or two amongst the islands, sleeping snugly in the boat's tiny cabin at night. The loch was big enough and sufficiently diverse in its topography that it was easily possible to find quiet spots where another human being could be neither seen nor heard. Rab loved the apparent remoteness of these locations, knowing that the hustle and bustle of normal life was not really that far away—and yet as distant as was necessary for a brief and treasured spell of peace and quiet.

Over the next few years, he set about a systematic exploration of the loch. The eastern shore was largely unspoilt and difficult to access from the land—a boat was the best way by far to get to it—and he enjoyed the sense of discovery that sailing there offered him. The myriad of islands provided even more areas of uncharted territory, presenting a seemingly infinite variety of locations to visit, each with its own characteristics and hidden secrets.

In his customary methodical way, he kept records of what he found and where he found it. Many of the places where he stopped had mementos of the previous habitation imprinted upon them—ruined castles, derelict cottages, and the remains of various small-scale industries which in the fullness of time had come and gone. He kept a log of his travels, with descriptions of what had caught his attention and why.

He stayed well clear of *InchPrior*, though. Although he had been given assurances that the *Faerie* would not trouble him again, he felt that discretion was still the better part of valour. Any time that he sailed in sight of it, he felt that he was being watched—though by what or by whom he could not say. To be fair he never thought that he was threatened in any way, just that he was being observed—and closely too. One day it would all get sorted out, but that day was still some time in the future.

Gradually, his records of the loch and its many islands began to amount to something fairly substantial, and he wondered a little if he should publish it all one day. It was not a proper scientific or cartographical survey, more a series of impressions and reflections on what he found in any one location. The physical attributes of each place were noted as carefully as he could—but there was something else which would be difficult to include in any publication.

Whenever he ventured out among the trees, inspected the occasional ruins on the islands, or sat quietly on a rock to look out over the water, he would calm his mind and let it float free to soar wherever it wished. The landscape, the water, the very air itself, all had a life and personality of their own. Just out of sight, just beyond hearing, he felt sure that there was another world—perhaps made up of memories of times past, perhaps of things to come—but either way a world of experiences presently unknown to him.

At night, tucked up in his berth aboard *Snowdrop 2*, he often dreamt of the forgotten lives connected with his immediate surroundings that day. Sometimes the impressions would be jumbled, or maybe just crowded with too much detail, but in time he found that he could more easily grasp the essence of the place—the *genius loci* if you will. His understanding of the languages that were spoken grew clearer, and on occasions, he imagined that he himself had become an integral part of what he saw and heard. It might be pushing things altogether too far to describe it all as some kind of alternative reality, but there were distinct moments in his dreams when he could practically taste the wood-smoke in the air, or feel the coolness of water droplets on his fingers, all as if he were indeed right there.

It was the regular annual summer holiday fortnight from work once again, and he decided that he wanted to spend more time alone on the loch. After several years of courtship, Ellie and Tam had now become engaged and were both taking on extra work in their spare time to earn extra money to help set up home together when they married. They no longer seemed free to go sailing with him anymore, and he accepted this change in their behaviour and habits with good grace. For his own part Rab was saving up to give them the best wedding present that he could manage, and he was, therefore, disinclined to head off to an exotic location for his summer break—somewhere that would cost him money that he could not spare.

A week exploring at his leisure aboard *Snowdrop 2* in this most beautiful of places seemed just fine to him. He planned to zigzag up the loch, stopping once in a while for a proper meal at one of the hostelries dotted around the shores, but each night sleeping on his boat—partly because he enjoyed it, and partly as an economy measure. Overnight stays at hotels and inns could prove expensive.

Rab gloried in a new technological invention that he had acquired! This was a small portable cassette player, easy to carry around when clipped to his belt. The model that he had chosen also had a radio, and he found that between his taped recordings and the daily broadcasts by the BBC, he could listen blissfully to wonderful music in the quietude of the evening after he had eaten his meal, or at any other time that he felt like it. He had built up a small collection of his favourite classics on tape, buying something new with each pay cheque. He now had all of the great violin concertos, with all of the greatest performers, and was exploring the vast symphonic repertoire of the late nineteenth and early twentieth centuries. He went through a lot of batteries!

Sailing conditions were good that summer and he island-hopped enthusiastically on *Snowdrop 2*, enjoying both the warmth of the sunshine and the gentle breezes which propelled his craft along. His skin grew dark from being outdoors so long each day, and his body became lithe and fit from the simple and regular exercise of sailing a small boat—leaping ashore to tie her up, and swimming in the clear water when the weather was warm and calm enough to do so.

Towards the end of his holiday, he was skipping between two large islands that lay about halfway up the loch when he felt a burning in the centre of his forehead, followed by an unfamiliar tingling on the back of his neck, something which caused the hairs there to stand on end. There were no signs of bad weather to be seen, even with his special sight, and yet…

He headed straight for the nearest scrap of dry land, a smallish island just big enough to sport a dark clump of trees. It was otherwise undistinguished and had no known name. He swiftly moored his craft, stepping ashore and walking away from the edge of the water as far as he could get. His hand in his pocket grasped the simple cigarette lighter that he now always carried with him. The spot on his brow burned ice-cold.

Even though it was the middle of the day, the light grew dim. A mist had risen from the surface of the water, climbing skywards until the island was completely enveloped in an impenetrable fog. Rab could see nothing, but he knew who was there alright. He waited.

"Rab, how you have grown! There is no dog now to warn you of our coming, yet you knew of it well enough without his help. Do not be afraid. You are easily strong enough these days to resist us if you wished—and you have absolutely no need of the fire that you keep hidden in your pocket!"

Rab could still see nothing, beyond a vaguely outlined shape or two in the gloom. There was more than one speaker, he was sure, but they merged seamlessly into a chorus that spoke musically and in perfect unison. There was no malice in the timbre of their collective voice, but that did not mean that he in any way trusted their intentions towards him. He was not afraid of them—but he still did not drop his guard.

"Why have you come? I sail these waters regularly, and since our past encounter on *InchPrior* you have never approached me, not until today that is."

"The *Traveller* has forbidden it until now. He will not influence the actual substance of any dialogue with you, Rab, but He has made it abundantly clear that we may not speak to you again until you are ready. We have been aware of His touch on you for many years now, and it shines from you like a glorious beam of light in a dark world. It illuminates—yes—but it also warns!"

Rab considered their words, but he thought past them to the things that lay beyond speech alone.

"I understand you better now," he said. "Our thoughts and feelings are not necessarily at odds with one other. They are just differently moulded and expressed."

"We have felt for some time, Rab, that things grow apart when they should be coming together. We are supple and changeable in our nature, with an ability to shift and manoeuvre as circumstances require—yet we cannot see any direction to it all. We travel with no known destination."

"I don't see these things any more clearly than yourselves," he replied, "and it may be that our shared blindness is, in fact, a deep well from which a better understanding may spring one day."

"Not everyone of your kind is of the same mind, Rab. In fact, you are somewhat unusual in your perception of these things. How do you see the future of this world? What progress can we make in moving forward?"

"Perhaps we should firstly reconcile our differences", he said, "and acknowledge our need for each other. Why else have we been thrown together in this way—in this place and at this time? Please understand that I feel no animosity towards you, only an uncertainty about your aspirations and your needs."

"Rab, we do not fear you now as we once did when we were able to see your hidden strength—but not your purpose or intent. We have felt exposed and vulnerable in this modern world of yours, and have need of someone from humankind who has insight and who can guide us on our path. If you help us to find our way, then we will, in turn, support you in yours."

It did not take Rab long to reply. "Agreed," he said.

Afar off, in the *Halls of the Immortals*, a smile swept across the face of one of the *Mighty*. "Well done, Rab!"

Chapter 17

The time came for Ellie and Tam to get married. They had decided to have the ceremony in a church close to where Tam had been brought up as a child. The venues for both the solemn religious part and the riotous celebrations which would inevitably follow were very near to each other, just across the street in fact. Good planning!

Earlier that year Rab had decided that it was time for him to buy a house of his own, somewhere that he could literally call 'home'. There were nice new-build houses beginning to appear in Balloch, and he had put aside enough money to place a deposit on one of them. He had also arranged to have the lease on his rented flat transferred to his sister and her husband-to-be. The owners in the big house were delighted, as in common with everybody else who had ever met them, they too liked the young couple.

Rab had felt prompted to time his move to that very year, as he had watched the pair search unsuccessfully in the area for somewhere simple and cheap in which to set up their own first home. His flat was modest but would suit the two newly-weds well for a while until they found their feet. His offer to pay their rent for the first six months as a wedding present was, in fact, the trigger that finally enabled Tam and Ellie decide to get hitched.

Rab could see that they really needed a place of their own if their relationship was to continue to hold together as well as to develop, even if their domicile was a bit on the small side. He had noted, however, in their frequent visits to him they had grown comfortable with his abode and would have no problems with moving in. He discreetly left them to make their own plans about how to furnish and decorate it.

At the wedding reception, Rab spoke briefly with his mother, but not at all to his father. Ellie looked a treat and was clearly very happy with her big day, and that was all that mattered to him. Rab was there for her and Tam, and that was enough.

It got hot in the hotel reception rooms, and he took the opportunity at one point to go outside for some fresh air. He was wearing his Granda's gold watch chain, but this time with a pocket watch that he had bought to go with it. The colour of the gold in the two items didn't quite match, but so what? It was the nearest that he could get to ensuring that his grandfather was there too.

The flower in his buttonhole had wilted a bit as the day wore on, so he discreetly dropped it in a litterbin by the door. He walked the short distance over to the church just to clear his head a little in the cool of the early evening and found a very smartly dressed guest standing by the gate, quietly looking into the silent graveyard. As he approached, Rab thought that he had not seen the man earlier in the day—perhaps he was a latecomer or a gatecrasher even!

"Rab! How nice to see you. The wedding's going well, and Ellie looks stunning, don't you think?"

Rab wasn't taken in for a moment. "Does anyone else know that You're here? Has anyone else seen You?"

"Now, you know that that's not very likely—not unless I've come for them, which I have not! It's *you* I hoped to have a chat with."

His sapphire blue eyes twinkled in the half-light of the fading day. Rab noticed the familiar shape of crossed wings, but this time worn as a floral decoration in the lapel of his jacket.

"Do you like that little touch? It was fun creating it. I wanted to celebrate too, you know, and to look the part should one of the *Others* be watching. Did I ever tell you how nosy they can get at times, especially when they think I'm up to something?

"Come, let's walk a little. If I play with things just a bit, no time will seem to pass in the outside world and nobody will even realise that you've been away. Would you like me to show you that wee trick sometime? Well, perhaps better not."

They strolled for what seemed to Rab like hours, stopping now and again to look at this or that. Rab noticed that the light didn't fade any further—but then it wouldn't, would it, if time had been suspended? The beautiful evening seemed to have no end or even the promise of an end.

They chatted about all sorts of things, to begin with, then moved on to the serious matters.

"Your time will come one day, Rab, as it must with all of your kind. It will not be soon by *your* way of thinking, and you will have time to have experiences and adventures enough before you are called. I will be there for you of course, but I would like you to think about where you want me to take you. Is there anything that you need to ask me?"

"Yes, there is. They say that the *Land of the Fair* is some kind of mid-way point between this world and the next one proper. What's it like?"

"I've been there many times, Rab, as you might gather, but it's never the same twice. It's not only the *Faerie* who shape-shift, their realm *Fairlinn* does so too. In fact, it contains many parcels of reality, quite different one from another, forming and dissolving again as required."

"As who requires?" Rab asked.

"Good question! When a spirit crosses over to spend time there, a pact or contract is drawn up to determine what is to happen to them. Conditions are created to permit—encourage even—progress towards a successful conclusion to their stay. Sometimes these conditions need to be reviewed.

"There are *guardians* who ensure that there are no digressions from the main purpose of the soul's visit—and make no mistake, a visit is all that it is. It is not a permanent destination for anybody. The *Faerie* allow travellers to stay with them only for a while and then eject them, either to go forward or back. They do not permit anyone to stay in limbo there forever. It's part of their pact with us."

"Should I go there?" Rab asked. "Will I benefit in some way? Why do the *Faerie* seem so keen to welcome me to their land?"

"I will not answer any of those questions for you, Rab. You are fully equipped now to do so for yourself. You have opened a dialogue with the *Fair Folk* and must discuss your terms with them yourself. I will not interfere."

They had stopped by the edge of the river and were watching the dark water flowing swiftly by. Rab looked down at the ever-changing currents.

"I feel somehow that we have become friends, you and I," he said. "Will that alter if I make the wrong decision about this?

I'll miss you if you walk out on me, you know. Can we not share a friendship, the two of us?"

"Whatever the decision is, Rab, it will be the right one—but only if it's truly *you* who makes it. I am flattered that you wish to be friends with me—make no mistake! People are fearful of me, perhaps with good reason, and often try to bribe me in an attempt to placate me, or win me over in some way. I don't ever remember anyone offering me their *friendship*, though, pure and simple and without strings."

The *Gatecrasher* considered deep within himself. "Rab, it's a glorious thing, friendship, but it can be weighty too and may imply commitment of sorts. However, if we can agree to make no demands on one another, and always try to see the other's point of view, then I would be proud to call you my friend."

They had returned to the churchyard, and after their long stroll, Rab suddenly felt a tad unsteady on his feet. Supporting himself briefly against the gate he turned to speak—but his visitor was no longer anywhere in sight.

A heady aroma of something really rather pleasant hung in the air. At Rab's feet lay a little spray of flowers, bound and crossed in the manner of two wings. He scooped it up gently and placed it on his lapel.

***

Rab returned to the celebrations. Ellie sidled up to him and caught his hand in hers.

"What a lovely buttonhole," she said, "and what a heavenly scent there is from it! I've been so busy up till now I didn't have time to notice it. That watch chain looks really posh! Will you not give me a dance, my dear? I saw you slip out a little while ago, and I thought that you were perhaps trying to avoid it!"

"I wouldn't miss it for the world, my sweet. I just needed a breath of air, that's all. What have you done with Tam? He hasn't done a runner already, has he?"

"He wouldn't dare! He knows I'd go to the ends of the earth to find him again, so there's no point in trying to escape, is there?"

Not for the first time, Rab's heart sang for the pair of them!

They danced a turn or two until Tam cut in and asked Rab with mock seriousness if it was alright if he had a dance with his new wife. He caught up with Rab later at the bar.

"I'm just beginning to realise what a deadly thing this marriage business is. I was thinking of organising a quick escape while the missus' back was turned. Any chance I could hide out on *Snowdrop 2* for a few days while I get my travel arrangements to Timbuktu sorted out?"

"No chance at all, Tam! She's seen us talking, and would figure it out in no time at all."

"Thought so! Well. I'd better just knuckle down to it then. After a few kids have arrived, she'll be so distracted that I'll be able to get to Timbuktu and back again before she's even noticed."

Don't count on it, thought Rab.

Chapter 18

In the years that followed, Rab continued to enjoy sailing out on the loch. *Snowdrop 2* became something of a second home for him, simple though she was. He loved heading off on this or that adventure, using the wind to propel him where it willed. His notes about his visits here and there grew extensive, and he thought more seriously about writing some kind of book about it all.

He had always had skills in art, and he now developed the technique of doing sketches in soft pencil, gently tinted with washes of watercolour. Sometimes he laid aside his pencil completely and worked exclusively with the brush. His initial attempts were fair enough—but only that. With practice, however, he greatly improved his ability to capture moods and innuendos, often neglecting mere detail in the interests of suggesting, rather than stating outright, what was actually there.

He took to packing his paints and sketchbook with him each time he ventured out on his boat and was never happier than when he could moor *Snowdrop 2* in some peaceful spot, put on his headphones, and drink in the sights which surrounded him.

He hoped that his images could be used with supporting text, not to produce some academic tome but preferably something that would reflect his own fascination with the ever-changing personality of this beautiful place. He was enchanted by the way that the light shifted throughout the day and totally fascinated by the cycle of the seasons over the year with its comings and goings of greenery and wildlife. He knew in his heart, though, that no matter how hard he tried to capture it all on paper, it was impossible to fix something that by its very nature was so fluid and mercurial.

Yet, by drawing and painting, he was indeed trying to define the indefinable. It was the eternal paradox of all art—otherwise, surely it would not be art but something else?

He did not himself have the financial resources to publish a work that to some people's eyes might appear a little esoteric. He tried without success to gain sponsorship of some kind, but everyone who saw his book wanted to change it to the kind of thing that they themselves might have wished to create, had they the skills. However, Rab was just not interested in doing other people's bidding on this one. He had something of his own to deliver, and if it was not good enough for this world, then he quite simply would not bother. They could write and illustrate their own book!

It was Jenny who came to his aid. She had made a point of staying in touch with him over the years, and he with her. She was getting old now but had never forgotten how he had befriended her sister when everyone else was going frantic with worry about how she would cope with her stroke. Jenny had inherited Sara's property and savings, and had also accumulated enough money after the death of her own husband to be considered rather well off, if not exactly rich.

"Now, I like your work," she said, "And Sara would have liked it too. If I stand behind you, so to speak, when you go to the publishers, can we agree that you pay me back as the returns mount? I attach only one condition, and that is that you mention her in your foreword somewhere."

The book was not exactly an international bestseller, but it did sell steadily in the local tourist shops. It was a lovely souvenir for visitors to buy as a memento and even got a reputation in the west of Scotland as an ideal present to give for birthdays or for Christmas. It never did quite cover its costs, though, but Jenny didn't give a damn. She loved Rab as the son she had never had, the son too that Sara had never had. He had never betrayed the trust that they had both placed in him, and she knew just how rare that was in this world.

On one of her little pre-arranged visits to Balloch, she popped in as usual to his house for a cup of tea and a good blether. She had never quite lost her habit of looking guilty when she dunked her biscuit in her tea, and Rab always had to suppress a smile and pretend to look the other way when she did so.

As usual, she did not mess about when she wanted to make a point. "When was the last time that you saw your friend with the winged hat? I think that it must be quite a while now."

"Yes, it was at Ellie and Tam's wedding. As usual, nobody noticed him except me, though he did leave behind a flower or two that people could actually see and smell. I'm not quite sure what happened to that buttonhole—it was there one minute and gone the next. Perhaps I shouldn't be surprised!"

He thought for a moment, then added, "The next sighting I have will be the last one, and will occur at my own death. I have no idea when that will be. I am to be ready, though, but for what I'm not really sure."

Jenny leant back in her chair and seemed to doze for a minute or two. She then opened her eyes.

"You have some years left in you yet, my dear, but I'm afraid that you will never see old age. I hope that it doesn't distress you to be told that. I don't normally predict deaths, and I'm not really going to do it with you. However, you need to get certain things straight in your head before it happens, and I don't feel that it is in your own interests to be caught unawares. You did say that He told you to be ready for Him, did you not?

"A young person is going to come into your life, and... Oh dear! I've just been blocked off! A veil has dropped down right over everything to do with this individual. Strange, that's never happened before. Perhaps I'm losing my touch? Odd!"

Rab sipped his tea and looked at her levelly. "I am not afraid of dying, Jenny, and He has promised me that it will not be stressful for me when it comes. I knew myself that I would never grow old, so you have not been unkind—truly. You have only confirmed what has been obvious to me for some time now. It does help me to prepare, though.

"I can't think who this young person could be. It's neither of Ellie's two children, I'm sure. I love them of course, but I can't see anything significant developing there. No matter."

The conversation moved on to other things, and Jenny expressed her satisfaction with the way things had gone with the book.

"I don't worry about the financial side of it, my dear. I'm just pleased that you produced something so beautiful, and in memory of Sara too. Everybody tells me how much they enjoy reading it."

"Oh Jenny," he said. "I miss her, and Smozo too. They were good friends to me. It would be wrong to say that I talk to them as if they were still here, but I do feel that they are watching me sometimes."

"That is because they are," said Jenny quietly.

Chapter 19

Time had drifted relentlessly by, and Rab now found himself in his late thirties. He was content with his lot as he had secured for himself the things that were significant to *him,* rather than the things that the rest of the world thought that he *ought* to find important. He didn't interfere in the lives of others, and he expected the same courtesy in return—even if he did not always get it.

More than one person came to regret tackling him on his apparent eccentricities—living on his own, listening to his 'strange' music, playing the violin, sailing away on the loch, and so on—and he could become quite cutting if they were unwise enough to cross a clearly defined line of demarcation. He took no prisoners if he felt that someone was being intrusive or just plain rude.

His knowledge of music was by now quite extensive and still growing. Particularly with his violin, he enjoyed exploring new territory and loved playing with other people in folk bands— partly for the camaraderie and partly for the exchange of ideas.

He had long since replaced his battered old instrument with one built by a good maker in Glasgow. He had appreciated being able to have a dialogue with the woman who crafted it for him, and it made him feel rather special to own and play something that had been created just for him. It was all good fun.

Snowdrop 2 had become like another limb, and at practically every opportunity, he sailed her out on the waters of the loch, even when the weather had turned a bit cold. He now felt quite safe and comfortable with visiting *InchPrior*, and the island became something of a favourite place to stop off. When he was there he often wondered just what had happened to the *Faerie Isle*—he could never see it, even though he knew that it was there somewhere.

Occasionally, though, he became distantly aware of a strange singing, just on the boundaries of his hearing, just on the edge of his consciousness. He thought of the *Faerie Folk*. Did their wondrous land have beautiful music to listen to and enjoy?

Perhaps, in fact, their realm was actually fashioned out of melody and song—now there was a thought! It would explain many things.

When on *InchPrior* he would often sit awhile in the graveyard, wondering about the people buried there and the kind of lives they had experienced. There were legends about an Irish saint who had come there in the 8th century—a daughter of the king of Leinster and a descendant of Arthur Pendragon himself. She had been a powerful influence in the area, and when she died, it was said that they laid her to rest under the altar of the little church she had built there. Not surprisingly, until the coming of the Reformation, it was something of a pilgrimage shrine—not in any international sense, of course, but for anyone passing by.

He found himself thinking about what sort of woman she was. How had she coped with the *Faerie*, whose dwelling lay so close to hers? Christian folklore was full of stories about Celtic saints who banished the *Fair Folk* to their own lands and imprisoned them there. Was this what they had meant on the *Isle of Mists* when they said that they felt excluded?

Rab was unsure. From the little that he had heard, he felt that St Kenna was indeed a sufficiently strong personality to face down the *Legions of Hell*, if that was how she saw them, but something didn't fit—didn't fit at all—and that was that *The Faerie Isle* was still there, despite her efforts to consign it to oblivion. What did all that mean then?

Quite clearly to Rab, the portal to the realm of the *Fair Folk* had never been completely sealed. The connection between their world and ours continued to exist. It could not be otherwise. He *knew* that there still had to be a bridge that crossed the divide, something that in more modern times had been neglected by humanity or quite simply forgotten. It was, however, a link which could obviously not have been abandoned totally. How else had the *Faerie* been able to come to him, and to speak with him?

Rab felt that it was going to rain that night. He was not expected at work the next day, so he had already decided to sleep aboard his boat, carefully tucked into one of *InchPrior's* tiny coves. As always, he had taken several days supplies with him just in case he got stuck anywhere, so he was easily able to cook a meal for himself. When he had eaten and cleared up, he settled down to listen to some music.

Brahms it was this time, full of rich autumnal colours and the flavours of abundant harvests. He loved the way that even when the music grew dark, there was always the inherent promise of a spring to come once winter was over. Rab had no fear of darkness or the night, knowing that it brought quietude and reflection and that it was always followed by the sweetness of dawn and impending renewal.

When eventually he grew drowsy, he crept into his sleeping bag just as the first drops of rain began to fall on the roof of the boat's cabin. He would sleep deeply that night, the gentle patter of water falling on the roof lulling him into a profound and satisfying slumber. In just a few moments, he had drifted gently away.

***

His dreams that night were remarkably lucid and clear. In them, InchPrior lay peacefully in an ocean of blue that brilliantly reflected the azure of an unclouded sky. The figure of a small woman stood by the shore, her head covered by a kind of hood that was fashioned as an extension of her cloak. She looked out over the loch, out towards a tiny island sitting not far offshore. She had become more settled over the years, but she could still burst into flames on occasion.

A sweet music stole over the water towards her, indefinable in its melodic structure and its tonality, but filled with such beauty that it could melt a heart of stone. She listened carefully, knowing where it was coming from, but not really caring what it meant.

All of her experience as a Christian woman and all of her training as a priestess of that religion taught her to deny and reject the calls for her attention that were sounding in her ears. She listened nevertheless.

111

Out of the music came the beginnings of shapes and meanings—unfamiliar to her and yet resonating with every fibre of her being. She considered.

"Come to me," she said imperiously. "I am a believer in the one true God, and I place my trust in Him. Come to me and do not be afraid."

Their answer came quickly. "What would you know about *truth* or about *God*, lady? What experience do you have of either? Do you imagine that we ourselves are unfamiliar with these greater things?"

She erupted, "It ill becomes you to be rude to *me*! I am of a line of kings on my father's side, and of a line of seers on my mother's. Your time here is coming to an end, *Fair Folk*, and you know it, as do I. Come to me, I say!"

They laughed. "You can refuse to understand us if you must—but it's *not* up to you to issue *us* with any commands! You know us in your heart, yet you choose to deny us. You are intent on shutting us out of your life, we can see, but the cost will be great. Take your convictions and nurse them well, priestess, because you will have need of them—for a time, at least. Without us, you will grow weak, and perish one day."

"As will you!" she retorted.

"At last, we find something on which we can both agree. You ask us not to be afraid of you—yet you are clearly afraid of *us*. We are no threat to anyone, except to those who seek to cross us."

They persisted. "Do not try to block us out, princess, or you will cut away a part of yourself at the same time. We know that the great days of your religion are yet to come, and over the next thousand years you will grow powerful and come to believe that you have defeated us, destroyed us even. Consider, though, that the more you deny *us*, the more you hurt *yourself*."

She drew herself up to her full height. "Do not parry words with *me*, Spirits of Darkness! I too have the *foretelling*, and know that you will fade to nothing in the light of God's word."

They hissed at her. "*Foolish woman!* You are blinded by your skills in prophecy, just as much as you are enlightened by them. You see one thing, only to ignore another. When you finally decide that you have eliminated us, *that* will be the very time that you too come to your own end.

"Religions come and go in this world—we have seen it times without number—and yours is no exception. Every one of them feels that it has insights that are denied to others. Every one of them treats outsiders as infidels and fools. We mock your arrogance and your shortsightedness! And yet we weep for it all too."

Kenna stood by the water's edge, silent and not moving. She remained for a long time, trembling with emotions unfamiliar to her. Their words had cut into her but had also simultaneously opened channels in her mind, conduits that had been there since childhood—forgotten, unused, and unexplored. It was true that she had abandoned the old ways of thinking, embracing her new religion with joy and with relish. It was also true that despite it all, she felt incomplete. She had lost as well as gained.

She was troubled and fought with herself, but after what seemed like an absolute age, she turned to them in quiet resignation. She spoke softly now.

"I am old now and will die soon. I am told that yours is a land where human souls can dwell for a time, to reflect on their past and future lives. At my death, I will come to you, as a Christian woman in the humility of my beliefs—and yet also in the hope that we may learn from each other. I will not abandon my God, but I wish to see and to understand more than I am permitted here in this life and in this place."

"Come, daughter of Eve. We await you."

Chapter 20

When Rab awoke the next morning, the rain had stopped, and in its place, there were splashes of watery sunshine which burst through the drifting clouds. He had slept well and felt completely refreshed. After eating breakfast, he sat sipping a mug of tea in the cockpit of *Snowdrop 2*, enjoying the changing light as it spilt over and around the loch.

He had enough experience of dreams by this time not to attempt to take them too literally. He accepted that they revealed their truths in oblique ways. He had no doubt that Kenna and the *Faerie* had never actually confronted each other directly quite in the way that he had dreamt, but he was equally sure that a confrontation of sorts *had* taken place.

He also knew that his dreams did not come to him at random, but always held some message or meaning for himself. Whatever had passed between Kenna and the *Fair Folk* was relevant to him too in some way.

The journey back home across the loch was pleasant enough, the wind blowing with just enough purpose to propel his yacht along at a brisk pace. After mooring her in her usual spot, Rab took the bus home, stopping along the way to pick up some basic shopping in the village store. He tended to acquire his other purchases in Glasgow when he was there working—a better choice of pretty well everything—but the local shops here were perfectly adequate for his more modest day-to-day requirements.

It was good to have a day off, now and again, when he could get on with caring for his garden or attending to household chores. There wasn't much for him to do that day, though, so he picked up his violin and launched into some new music that he had promised to play at a local function in about a week's time. It wasn't really that difficult, but its unfamiliarity did present something of a challenge for him.

In the middle of his practice, the doorbell rang. He wasn't expecting anybody and, slightly irritated at being interrupted, he went to answer. He had little patience with hawkers or door-to-door salesmen, and he opened the door fully prepared to chase his caller away with as little ceremony as possible.

On his doorstep stood a very attractive young girl just entering the fullness of her womanhood. Somehow she looked familiar, although equally, he was sure that he had never seen her before.

She looked at him directly in the face, and with a mischievous smile said in a soft American drawl, "Hello, father."

Rab stared at her stupefied. *"WHAT!"* he said.

"Are you going to keep me standing here all day long, or are you going to invite me in for coffee—or as I suspect in these parts, some tea? Mom sends her regards."

Rab picked himself up from the floor and gestured inside.

"My name is Rosanna," she continued. "It's a blending of your own name with mother's—Robert and Anja. I arrived yesterday and asked around until I found you—we had heard that you were still here somewhere."

"I have coffee if you would like," said Rab, "but I'm notoriously bad at making it. Would you like to attend to that yourself, so that it's actually fit to drink? I'll stick to tea."

She laughed and said that she would fix his tea as well. Rab sat down—he needed to! He thought back to his teenage days when Anja had told him that she would be leaving for America with her family. He remembered their fond farewells—and just how fond they actually were!

Rosanna returned with the tea and coffee. Completely unfazed by being in someone else's house for the first time, she had gone on a raid while in the kitchen and found some biscuits hiding in a tin.

"I suppose I had better fill you in on a thing or two," she said. "When the family arrived in the States, nobody knew that mother was pregnant—though she was aware of it herself. Before it all became too obvious, she ran off to a cousin living in Boston, someone who had fallen out with the rest of the family and was no longer speaking to any of them."

"I heard that she had disappeared at one stage, but that was all the news I ever had." Rab ventured. He was still in shock.

115

"Mom was careful about letting too much get out and hid away while I was being born. With help from her cousin, she was able to keep me with her while she took employment, first of all as a receptionist in a large office block, and then as the PA for the boss of the company himself."

"That sounds like her alright," said Rab. "I can't imagine Anja going unnoticed or unappreciated for long!"

Rosanna laughed. "I'll tell her you said that! In fact, she caught the eye of the boss's son, Chuck, and he asked her to marry him—with me in tow, too! I have two little brothers now, and we all get along just fine. Chuck adopted me as his own, and when I turned eighteen he gave me a generous allowance so that I could have a bit of independence. It was his idea, rather than mother's, that I came to look for you. She wasn't at all sure how you would take it."

"I'm not sure myself!" he replied. Rab was still totally winded.

"What am I to call you?" she said. "*Dad* or *Pa* doesn't seem right somehow."

He thought for a moment. "We never knew each other as parent and child, and it sounds that you already have a father to be proud of. Why not just call me *Rab* like everyone else? By the way, where are you staying? Have you come alone? Would you like to move in here for a while? I think that we have a lot of questions to ask each other."

She stayed for the best part of a week until her flight home was due. They both had great fun paying a surprise visit to Ellie and Tam, and meeting the kids—her cousins in fact. Everyone got along famously, and Ellie volunteered to take Rosanna to meet her grandparents, knowing that Rab would not cross their threshold for all the tea in China.

Rosanna wanted to visit all the places that her mother had known—the school, the family house, even the park where she suspected she had been conceived. Gently, she asked about Smozo and listened carefully to Rab's stories about the little dog. Anja would want to know every detail.

One evening, after dinner, when they were sitting in Rab's living room, Rosanna began to look serious and shifted a little in her seat.

"Mother wondered if you would be able to help me with something. I often have strange dreams, and sometimes see things that others are entirely unaware of. The night I arrived here in Balloch, I dreamt I was standing on the shores of a lake— I presume Loch Lomond—looking out to a tiny island nearby. I know it sounds crazy, but I was talking to it, and it was answering me. I couldn't make any sense of what was being said though. Mom thinks that this all comes from your side of my parentage, and has to do with the *second sight*."

It took Rab only a moment to realise that they had both been having a near-identical dream at precisely the same time. What could all this mean?

"Do you ever see a handsome man, always wearing some kind of winged decoration on his head?" he asked.

"Why yes! How did you know that? I've never told anybody, in case they thought I was hallucinating and should be put away—not even Mother!"

"I think that we should visit *InchPrior* together. Can you sail? We can talk about it all on the way. We can easily get there and back in one day."

And the next time I see my heavenly friend, I'll put a flea in his ear about playing games with me!

Chapter 21

Rosanna thoroughly enjoyed her time in Balloch. She got on just famously with Ellie and her family—and of course, the kids absolutely adored her, and wanted to know when she was coming back! She even managed to charm Rab's parents in a way that he never had. Visiting *InchPrior* proved to be a little bit more difficult for her, though.

She had been taught to sail by Chuck, and Rab noted with approval how well she handled *Snowdrop 2*. They skimmed along the edge of the islands at the southern end of the loch until they came to *InchPrior* itself. Rab moored in the natural harbour at the north end of the island and they stepped ashore. Rosanna looked distinctly ill at ease.

"Whatever was in your dream," Rab said, "it cannot harm you now. Was there some unpleasantness that you don't like to think about?"

"It is not the dream that bothers me—it's actually being here that gives me the creeps. I feel I've been here before, but that just isn't possible, is it? It all seems so familiar. Where is the *Faerie Isle*, though? You did say that it could come and go, did you not? I just get the sense that I'm being watched by something or somebody."

It struck Rab that she seemed a bit confused, troubled in some way. Her words were tumbling over one other, and she was close to incoherence.

"I always think exactly the same when I'm here, but it no longer gives me grief," Rab observed. "Are you frightened of something?" He wondered if she was thinking of Kenna.

"I know it sounds stupid, but I feel that some kind of drama unfolded here in the past—and maybe it's left a shadow of some kind behind. I can practically taste it. Just give me a moment while I confront whatever it is."

She stepped over to the shore and looked out across the water. She breathed deeply and slowly and then felt a great calmness come over her while her mind settled. Rab's presence strengthened her—just knowing that he was there stiffened her resolve and bolstered her self-assurance. After a short while, she smiled quietly, thoughtfully even. Then as she turned away a flash of pain crossed her face, then cleared just as quickly as it had come.

"It's done," she said. "Whatever it was that needed to be achieved here is over and done for me now. Thank you for bringing me, but can we go now?"

They sailed the short distance to Balmaha and stopped at the village inn for some lunch. There was a buzz of conversation from the other people there—a group of ramblers mostly, with a smattering of others who had driven around the loch for a lazy day by the water's edge. They managed to find a table in a corner, away from the general melée and sat without speaking while they waited for their food to arrive.

In time a hearty lunch appeared on their table. Hungry after all that fresh air, they tucked in with enthusiasm.

"What was it you saw that troubled you?" Rab asked. "You seemed distracted for a moment."

Rosanna hesitated. Almost reluctantly she answered, "I saw more than one thing, but at one point I did see your death there, down by the shore. I don't know *when* it will be, but it will be there, certainly. The shadow I mentioned was to do with your loss, I think, rather than for anything else experienced there before.

"It *felt* like the past, though, and that's new for me. I've not sure I've seen the past before—or the future, come to think of it. I just see the *present* a bit differently from other people."

She followed through, "How can that be? How can something that's not yet happened leave a memory of itself?"

Rab answered, just a bit ruefully. "If you've had even the briefest of experiences of the *Trickster*, you will have learnt that time can do strange things. People with our talent can tune into events past, present, and future, and it's not always easy to determine which one it is. Perhaps in *our* way of seeing things, time is slippery and difficult to pin down at times."

She looked slightly puzzled, then suggested, "They say everything is cyclic, but that can't be quite right, can it? Things can come around again, I know, but never in exactly the same way. We do move on, don't we?"

Rab thought for a moment. "Think of it as a bicycle wheel. When it's moving on the road, each point on the rim turns around the hub and after one revolution comes back to where it started—relative to the hub, that is. However, both the wheel and the hub have travelled on, and are themselves no longer in the same place."

"I like your analogy," she replied. "It explains why there was a sense of familiarity on *InchPrior*, a feeling that I had been there before. It also explains why it felt different too. This all doesn't seem to trouble you."

"I noticed it a very long time ago. It was something that my Granda taught me. I was very young and had just become aware of the passage of the seasons. I became fascinated by the springtime and the sudden bursting of life that it brought with it. Granda said that no matter how many times I experienced it, no matter how familiar it all might become, it would still always seem wonderfully fresh and new—the same but different too!"

Rab paused in his thoughts for a moment or two. "Did you connect in any way with Kenna?"

"Yes, but only very briefly. For just a little while, it seemed that I *was* her, looking out towards the *Fairy Isle*. I could feel her thoughts, but it all passed so quickly. You know, sometimes I think that I make that kind of connection just a bit too closely for comfort. It's not the first time that I've found myself sucked so powerfully into someone else's emotions that I feel them as if they were my very own. I don't think it affects you in quite the same way, though."

"No, it doesn't. Perhaps it's a female thing!"

Rosanna smiled mysteriously, and delicately finished her cappuccino.

"Not bad," she said, licking her lips. "Mom always thought that the coffee here was terrible—but I think that maybe it's caught up with the rest of the world! I wonder, though, if the rest of the world will ever catch up with *you*. I just can't talk to anyone else the way that we do with each other. I've had to wait a long time for this."

Rab smiled. "None of it ever came smoothly for me either, I assure you. If I can make it easier for you, and spare you some of the pain, I will. It always strikes me as a terrible irony that they call it a *gift*—a curse more like, not to see the world as others do. It isolates you."

"Did your Granda have the skill? They say that it's inherited—but then we both know that, don't we?"

"Yes, I'm sure he did. He would have been able to help me had he lived, but I barely knew him before he was gone. The *Sight* can skip generations, you know. Sometimes it runs uninterrupted for hundreds of years, and then there is a gap. I don't know why."

"Has *He* been able to help? I've seen Him from time to time too, as we know, but He never talks to me like he does to you."

"I suppose it depends on what you mean by *help*. At first, He never spoke, and I was about the age you are now when I first heard Him say anything at all. Yes, I suppose He has helped in his own way. I wonder, though, if He is himself unsure of us— or perhaps more accurately, unsure about his *relationship* with us.

"He did say on one occasion that some things were kept even from *Him*—and that struck me as being odd for someone we think of as being divine. Perhaps, like ourselves, He is but a part of the totality of things and has to find his own way as well. He's just a bit of a scallywag too, and I wonder sometimes how representative he is of what the *Others* think and do."

Rosanna paused for a moment or two. "Do you feel that He has enemies?"

"Yes, I do. I have no knowledge or understanding of who or what that might be, but it has occurred to me more than once that He's wary of something at times. He hides it well, but it's there nevertheless."

"Do you think that He'll talk to me too one day?"

"Inevitably! It seems to be part of his way of doing things that He lets us see him first, and only afterwards decides whether both parties are ready for some kind of dialogue—but that implies uncertainty of some kind, does it not, a lack of cast-iron inevitability?"

Rosanna went all thoughtful again. "Yes—and it calls into question what we actually mean by *divinity*—all-knowing, all-seeing?"

"Absolutely! I have thought about it many times, but have learnt to be content with an awareness of the *question*—the answer is something else, surely! Perhaps that can never be fixed to the floor, never pinned down, never actually defined."

He warmed to his theme. "Every time I hear someone pontificate about their religion; every time someone tries to explain to me where I have gone wrong in life; every time they try to convert me in one way or another to their own beliefs— it's at all of those times that I most want to walk away. I don't think divinity can be limited by *our* meagre perceptions, no matter who we think we are. It's quite simply too big. We can touch a part of it, though."

Rosanna turned to him, her pretty face flushed with affection. "Rab, I wish I could spend more time with you, but I need to get back to my family and pick up the threads of my life there. Chuck was right to get me to come here, even if it's only for a short time. He's a great guy, you know, but there's just no way we could ever have this kind of conversation together."

"He has done you proud, nevertheless. I'll probably never meet him, but I admire and respect him for everything that he is. Your mother was lucky to find him."

Rosanna laughed. "He says that *he* is the lucky one!"

Rab paid up, and they made their way back around the loch. He was careful to take *Snowdrop 2* around *InchPrior* on the *other* side of the island this time—but the feeling of being watched was still there.

Chapter 22

Two years had passed since Rosanna's visit. They corresponded regularly, but Rab knew in his heart that they would never meet again in this life. He also knew that there would be many other things that he would not see again in this world—or in the next one either.

They managed to keep him out of pain—for which he was grateful. There was a vagueness about how long they expected him to survive and his guess was as good as theirs, perhaps even a good bit better.

He made his plans. He decided not to discuss any of it with his family or friends. That might appear cruel to some, but he didn't want to put them all through the agony of watching him slowly rot to death in a hospital bed. His way was surely kinder all around.

It wasn't difficult to sort out his affairs and to apportion what he had amongst his family. Everything was to be divided up and given to the generation below him—to those who still had to make their own start in life. They, or their guardians, were to decide for themselves how to deal with the money matters—and of course with *Snowdrop 2*.

He did take care to remember Rosanna in his will, but he knew that she would be well provided for in the States, no matter what. Almost as an afterthought, he made a change that allowed her to take possession of his house—but only if she wished. Rather than leave absolutely everything to her, he made generous provision for Ellie's children too so that one day they too could have the chance of something better.

He wrote an individual letter of farewell to everyone, to arrive after the event, telling them how much he had loved them and how he had wanted to spare them the trials of a slow passing. His letter to Rosanna was the one that caused him the most tears. It was cruel to meet his daughter the way he had, and then see her walk out of his life again. On the other hand, he was grateful for the opportunity to have met her at all.

When all was ready, he decided that it was the right time to put his plans into action. He was just beginning to show the external signs of his illness, and wouldn't be able to hide it from the world for much longer. It was now or not at all. He took care to conceal any hint of what he intended to do and left his house in as normal a fashion as he could for one last sail on the loch. The weather was fair that day, and he followed his usual routine of taking the bus around to where he kept *Snowdrop 2* moored, stopping for half an hour or so in the café by the water's edge for a quick bite to eat and his usual cup of tea.

Rab paid up and exchanged his customary little pleasantries with the staff before walking down the jetty. There were just a few people about—a man standing several feet out in the water fishing; some children playing with a ball; an elderly couple strolling along arm-in-arm with their frisky little dog running along beside them.

He began to untie his boat from the jetty and climbed aboard.

"Hang on! Am I not coming too, Rab?"

He turned, recognising the voice. "I wondered at what stage we'd meet. You had your back to me as I came by, and I didn't realise who it was. The fishing gear suits You."

"Do you really think so? You don't reckon that the waders are a bit over the top? I thought I'd get my feet wet otherwise."

Rab searched for the wings for a moment or two and then found them.

"That's quite a hairstyle You've got there. I nearly missed the wings, but I see You've got them beautifully coiffured into Your curls!"

"Oh shucks! I'm all embarrassed now! I just thought it was a bit classier than a tattoo. People won't talk, will they?"

"People always do. Incidentally, since You're here I assume that I've got the timing right?"

"That was always up to you, anyway, right from the beginning—but you did manage to catch us all a little by surprise. You've always been a bit difficult to read—it's just a part of what you are, Rab! We weren't really expecting you to jump the gun like this. Have you decided where you want to go?"

124

"Yes. I would like to spend some time in the *Land of the Fair*."

"Fine! There's no rush, so let's take the scenic route."

The boat finished untying its restraints all by itself; the sails were hoisted by unseen hands, and off they swept away from the shore.

"Just relax. I'll do the steering—I'm really quite experienced, you know. Did I ever tell you how I helped Jason sail the *Argo* to Colchis to find the Golden Fleece? Oh well, perhaps another time!"

To anyone watching, the little yacht sailed calmly and serenely out over the water, completely untroubled by contrary wind or waves. Nobody really noticed her of course, as they never did unless *He* wanted them to. To Rab's surprise, they turned and headed north, away from his intended destination on *InchPrior*. This must be what was meant by the *scenic route*.

Rab sulked for a moment, and then spat it out, "You didn't tell me about Rosanna. That wasn't very nice! I thought we were friends. Is that what friendship means in your book?"

"You didn't enjoy my little joke? No, I don't suppose you saw it that way! We just needed to keep you two apart in the early stages. Things would have got unnecessarily complicated otherwise."

"Who's *we*?"

"Now that would be telling! Maybe it's just the royal plural—on the other hand, maybe it's not. You're not going to give me a ticking off about it, are you? I know a petted lip when I see one!"

"It's *not* a petted lip. I was just trying not to bare my teeth!"

"Oh—that bad, eh? I'm sorry if that makes you feel any better. Like everyone else in existence, I sometimes have to do things I don't always like. It was the only way, you know. By the way, what's a *scallywag*? I don't ever remember hearing that word when you lot do yon worship thingy you're all so fond of."

Oops! thought Rab. *I wonder what 'touché' is in OlympianSpeak.*

He decided that he was not going to get anywhere on the issue of Rosanna, so perhaps he should let it go. He still wasn't pleased, though.

"Good," said the *Steersman*. "That little exchange got us over the difficult bit. I find that people get just a bit upset when we make that particular jump. It was better that I diverted your attention for a few moments."

"What do you mean, '*particular jump*'? Am I dead already?"

"No, but there *is* a dramatic change of view! If you would just stop glowering at me and look around you, I think you'll see what I mean. We're sailing around the Milky Way—well, sort of sailing! Did you know that it got that name because it was supposed to be spillage from the breasts of *Hera* herself? She finds that quite hilarious, and wonders how people could be so naïve. Now, just look at the colours of that over there!"

Rab was mesmerised by the sheer beauty of his surroundings. Never in his wildest dreams had he ever imagined that one day he would be floating across the firmament in this way. He was speechless with wonder. The universe was just so utterly lovely.

"Now you mustn't think that just because it's *beautiful*, it's *friendly* too! Much of what you're looking at would be absolutely deadly to your kind, and it would be better if you never tried to go there. I know that humankind dreams of travelling out amongst the stars—but just keep on dreaming and don't actually attempt to do it!"

Rab sat transfixed. He was full of questions. "It's breathtaking, it really is! Are there other worlds out there? What sort of inhabitants do they have? Will we *never* get the chance to visit them? Do they know about *my* world? How—*oh never mind!* You wouldn't tell me anyway, or at least not in any way that I could understand."

As the panorama unfolded, Rab had a sense of mighty events that had taken place in the past, and yet were still happening today. He saw worlds being created and then destroyed, great civilisations rise and fall, individual creatures live their lives and then expire. He was aware of the vastness of the timeframe and yet felt that it was all passing within the compass of a single breath. He was quite overwhelmed, and sat in stunned silence.

All of a sudden he felt weak, his energy completely spent. The view shifted back to one of normality—whatever that was! The *Steersman* turned the boat's tiller, and they changed tack a point or two.

"Look, there's our destination. We've returned home again. We were just a tad early, and I needed a distraction while we got some things sorted out—behind the scenes so to speak. That wee tour of the Milky Way did the trick just fine! We'll trim sail a bit and get ready for our arrival. They're expecting us, you know!"

Rab turned, and in doing so caught sight of *InchPrior*, bathed in sunshine afloat a perfect sea. Soon now!

He looked once again back towards his passenger, only to find him gone—or was He?

Larger than life, the figure of a beautiful man stood poised over the water. He smiled reassuringly at Rab.

"The time is now with us, my friend. When people come to it, it's always easier than they think—even if the run-up can be a bit unpleasant at times.

"You will feel a shadow pass over you—though only very briefly—and then we can move on. Look! They've opened the gateway for us."

Rab raised his head, which had begun to droop wearily down onto his chest. Below the graveyard and over a tiny islet with a pattern of stones set upon it, a wondrous rainbow had appeared. It was almost a complete circle, with only the merest portion cutting down below the surface of the water. Through it, he could see figures looking out towards him. Was that a quayside with buildings he could see too—on such a small island?

"My sister *Iris* likes to play with rainbows, you know. She does things with them that your people would find quite alarming. Gently does it now!"

Momentarily, Rab felt a coolness on his brow as if softly brushed by a tiny crystal of ice. A shadow passed across his eyes, and in an instant, it was all over.

Chapter 23

They found *Snowdrop 2* tethered to a rock, offshore from *InchPrior*. Everything aboard her was properly stowed, and her sails were furled neatly and purposefully, as if ready for immediate use. What she was doing there—and how her crew had departed without the assistance of another vessel—was a complete mystery.

Of Rab, there was no sign.